RIDDLES & RICHES

VEGAS CHANTLY MYSTERIES

BOOK 2

KYLE OWENS

CHAPTER 1

THE MORNING SUN slipped from behind the far hills that overlooked the Pine Sap Camper Park. At campsite twenty-one, a silver Airstream with Woody Woodpecker painted on the side sat quietly beneath a shadow of trees. A radio clicked on somewhere inside its thin walls.

"Good morning, Georgia. In the news today: gas prices and inflation fears are surging once again. New York Publishing giant Read a Book Publishers is about to be acquired by the even bigger World Media. A strand of Richard Nixon's hair was sold at auction for two dollars and forty-nine cents. The anonymous buyer is reported to have a huge Richard Nixon memorabilia collection. If I had a Richard Nixon collection, I'd want to be anonymous, too. The weather forecast calls for partly cloudy skies with a fifty percent chance of pop-up thunderstorms this evening with a high of ninety-one. So be sure to crash any pool party in your neighborhood."

Vegas Chantly stretched out her arm from under the sheet and reached out and turned off the radio. She laid there for a few seconds trying to wipe the sleep from her eyes before she pulled the sheet down slowly and stared up at the ceiling. Stuck to it was a bumper sticker that read, "I like soup beans so you better stay back," which she had placed there on a family camping trip when she was seven years old. She sat up slowly and jumped back in surprise when she saw her mother standing over her. Eleanor Chantly wore a trench coat and had a large purse slung over her shoulder, and she looked upset.

"Well, I'm banned from the DMV," Eleanor said.

Vegas groaned. "Mom, why do you keep breaking into my camper and scaring me to death?"

"First of all, I didn't break into your camper. I used my key."

"At least let me know you're around by making a noise first. It's scary waking up to somebody in your house that you weren't expecting."

"I'm not trying to scare you. I'm trying to tell you my problems."

"That scares me, too."

Eleanor sat down on the edge of Vegas' bed with a worried look on her face. "How am I going to get around if I can't drive? I guess I'll have to buy a horse or a wheelbarrow or something."

"What are you talking about?"

"I went to the division of motor vehicles yesterday to renew my driver's license and they told me to leave."

"That happens everywhere you go," Vegas pointed out.

"They can't ban me from getting a driver's license, can they? I paid all of my taxes. At least, I think I did. I don't have any tickets. I did back into the corner of the house yesterday. I was going to take the mattress out and put in a new one. So I backed up to the house to make it easier to get the new mattress in and the old one out, then I heard a loud bang. I can't believe I did that."

"Well, a two-story house is hard to see. Why didn't you call me to help you?"

"I thought I could do it. I was right, by the way. The

mattress is fantastic. The corner of the house isn't. But my vehicle is fine. Do you think that's why they wouldn't let me get a driver's license?"

"Let me see your driver's license."

Eleanor reached into her large purse and began flailing about. She rummaged around and pulled out a multi tool, several greeting cards, and a box of chocolate-covered cherries.

"How much stuff do you have in that purse?"

"Just the important stuff," said Eleanor. "It's like my Batcave in here. When the commissioner calls, I'm ready." She finally found her license and handed it to Vegas. Her daughter stared at it and shook her head.

"Your license doesn't expire for another four years."

Eleanor took the license back and looked it over. "You're kidding. I thought it was due this month."

"The month is right, but the year is wrong. Now the DMV can be dreading you coming back every day for the next four years."

Vegas crawled out of bed and sat on the edge of it beside her mother. She rubbed her eyes, then stared at her mother's trench coat.

"Why are you wearing a trench coat on a day when it's supposed to be in the nineties?"

Eleanor quickly stood and opened it up and showed it off to Vegas as if she was a *Price is Right* model. "Do you like it? I bought it at Willard's. They had it on sale, and it comes with a hat."

Eleanor dug into her right coat pocket and pulled out a hat, then yanked it on her head until it was low on her forehead, almost covering her eyes. "How do I look?"

"You look like Dick Tracy's overdressed mother. Can you see out from under that hat?"

Eleanor took the hat off. "Not really. It is a couple sizes too big for me. But when I wore it out of the store, people were pointing at me, so it definitely had an impact on society."

"Why did you buy that?"

"I'm a detective now. This is what all detectives wear, you know."

"You're not a detective. You're a problem."

"Here, try it on."

"I don't want to try it on."

Before Vegas could move away, her mother grabbed her, and in a matter of seconds, had taken off her trench coat and put it on her daughter. She then slammed the hat on top of her head and stared at her.

"You look like a private investigator now. The world had better be prepared for wow now when you walk into the room. You look like a Dick Tracy."

"And you're one of my villains, Mama Big Coat."

Vegas took the coat off and handed it back to her mother along with the hat. "I've got things to do today. So why don't you go on back to your Batcave and help Robin get his cape out of the wheel spokes of the Batcycle."

"What do you have to do today? I can help."

"No, you'll just get in the way."

"Is it another case?" Eleanor asked with the enthusiasm of a child who wanted to see the shark tooth again.

"No, I don't have another case, and even if I did I don't want you to get involved in it with me."

"But we're a great team. We solved the last one together."

"Not this time, Mom. It's too dangerous. I keep telling you that," Vegas said as she began making herself some coffee. "By the way, where's Buttermilk?"

"I let my cousin Nadine have him. She has seven kids and she promised them a dog, so I let him go to her. Since he's a basset hound, he's long enough that all the kids can pet him at the same time."

"Seven kids?" Vegas shuddered.

"Yeah, that's a lot. You know, I don't really remember ever seeing her husband. Of course, I guess she probably killed him by now. I mean seven kids and all is a lot."

"Do you think you could have raised seven kids?"

Eleanor frowned. "No. No, I would not have been able to raise seven kids. I mean the money alone to pay for them all would be stressful enough. Your father came from a big family, though, so he probably would have liked to have had a big family. Your father was an animal in the bedroom."

"Mom!" Vegas shouted as she put her hands over her ears. "I don't want to hear things like that or I'll be in therapy for a hundred years."

"Well, it's true," said Eleanor with a wicked grin as she put the trench coat back on and placed the hat on her head. "By the way, where's your red car?"

Vegas sat down with her cup of coffee. "I had to take it back."

"But you and that car were perfect for each other. Like the best buddies in the world."

"We were that, but the payments weren't."

"I would have helped you pay for it. Why didn't you let me do that? That's what moms are for. We don't just drive our kids crazy, we also help them drive themselves." Eleanor seemed to surprise herself with her words. "Hey, that's pretty good, if I say so myself."

"I'm a grown woman now. I have to pay my own bills."

"Don't you worry, I'll drive you to all your cases. Being that my driver's license is still good, I can drive you to all your cases for the next four years. You can thank your DMV for that."

"No, Mom, Pepper is going to bring a car by today for me to try out. If I want it, he said I could pay it off a little at a time."

The payphone outside rang and Vegas got up and hurried to it. Eleanor ran outside with her, shouting, "Why don't you get a cellphone instead of this payphone?"

"Because I don't forget where this payphone is," Vegas said as she stood at the payphone, took a deep breath then picked up the phone. "Vegas Chantly, P.I. How may I help you?"

On the other end of the line was a man's voice. "Yes, this is Davis Harper, publisher of Read a Book Publishers. I was wondering if you were available for a case."

"I can look at my schedule and possibly work you in."

Eleanor took that as her cue. "Ms. Chantly, this is your secretary. You are swamped with very important clients. Are you sure you want to take on another case?"

Vegas looked at her mother horrified and placed her hand over the phone speaker and whispered, "What are you doing?"

"I'm making you sound important," Eleanor whispered back. "Like a girl on the go."

"I need you to go away," Vegas whispered back.

"So you're good here?"

"I talk better on the phone alone."

"Gotcha. If you need me, I'll be in the camper," Eleanor whispered, then kissed her daughter on the cheek and walked away.

Vegas turned her attention back to the potential client. "What do you need?"

"My company is about to be acquired, and the company and I need to ... well, maybe it would be best to talk to you in person. Could I come by your office today?"

Vegas glanced up at her mother, who had somehow shut the camper door on her trench coat and couldn't get free.

"Uh, maybe it would be better if I just come by your office instead. Things are really kind of crazy around here."

"Well, I'm from New York and I'm here on a business trip. Maybe we could meet at a mutual location."

"That'll be fine."

"I'm just outside the Reno Café. Do you know where that is?"

"Oh, sure, I can meet you there. I eat there all the time. I should be there within thirty minutes."

Vegas watched Eleanor pull her coat loose from the door and fall to the ground like a sack of potatoes thrown from a train. Vegas whispered at her, "Are you okay?"

"I was until I fell down," Eleanor yelled back as she sat up and began dusting herself off.

"What was that?" asked Mr. Harper.

"It's nothing. It was just the office janitor. He accidentally stepped into his mop bucket."

"I see. Well, I'll see you in thirty minutes then."

"I'll be there," Vegas said and hung up the phone. Her mother walked to her trying to straighten out her coat and picking off dirt grains from the fabric.

"Who was that?" asked Eleanor.

"Mr. Harper. He's a publisher in New York."

Eleanor immediately was in awe. "You got a call from a publisher? They want to see your autobiography. Oh, my goodness, I'm going to be famous."

"I didn't write an autobiography."

"You wrote a children's book?" asked Eleanor with a great deal of excitement. "I am so proud of you. Am I in it?"

"Oh, yeah, you're the witch."

Eleanor frowned but then brightened. "I'd rather be the queen, but a witch is good, too. Do I get to fly around with some flying monkeys?"

"Mom, I didn't write a children's book," said Vegas, surprised that her mother actually thought she had.

"You should write a book about all of your adventures. But you don't seem to write much of anything."

"That's because I'm always too busy trying to help you up. Are you okay, by the way?"

"I'm fine. I might not be able to throw the football for a couple days, but I'll be okay. Say, do you have to go to New York?"

"No. I just have to go to the Reno Café."

"He left New York to come here and get a cup of coffee?"

"I'm not exactly sure what he wants. But I need to go and meet him because he's waiting for me. I need to borrow your car."

"No."

"What do you mean no? I have to get there now, and I don't have a car."

"Mommy will drive you there."

"No, Mom, every time you go with me, something happens that ends up with me telling you to be still and I'll get it off."

"I'm driving you to your meeting," Eleanor said adamantly. "Besides, it might not be safe."

"It'll be safe as long as I don't eat the ham."

Eleanor walked to the driver's side door of her SUV while taking off her coat and hat. "Come on and let the wicked witch drive you."

"I can't believe this," said a frustrated Vegas. "When do I get to live an independent life?"

"Mommy will make sure you're independent."

"How are you going to do that when you're always with me?"

"I'll let you pay for the gas."

CHAPTER 2

ELEANOR PULLED up in front of Reno Café and drove onto the sidewalk as she was trying to park. She had to back up, then move forward a couple of times to get it positioned properly. The two got out, and Eleanor admired her parking abilities.

"That didn't take too long for mommy to park, did it?"

"I noticed everybody rushing to their windows to watch you," said Vegas.

"They obviously wanted to watch a professional parker show them how it's done."

"I believe they were wondering why a blind woman was driving."

Eleanor stared lovingly at her SUV. "Do you think I should name my vehicle?"

"Name it? Why?"

"I don't know," Eleanor said as she humped her shoulders. "Just to show it affection, I guess. Maybe it will try harder when I go to park if it has a name. Oh, I got it. I'll call her Miss Rosie."

Vegas stared at her mother. "That sounds like the name of a housekeeper."

"Miss Rosie it is," Eleanor said as she patted her vehicle lovingly on the door. "Now when I go park, I'll just tell Miss Rosie to take it easy and help mommy."

"They make vehicles now that can park themselves."

"I'm not driving one of those things," Eleanor said while wagging her finger. "When I get into the driver's seat, I'm doing the driving."

Vegas stared at the SUV and said, "Poor Miss Rosie. You'll have her screaming all the time."

"I don't trust vehicles that can drive themselves. I might end up somewhere I didn't mean to be going. I've also decided something else."

"What's that?"

"I don't like the name Miss Rosie. It's not action-sounding enough to me."

"You could call it Crash."

Eleanor frowned. "I'm not going to call it Crash. Sometimes I think you believe I'm just a crazy old woman that you're going to have to put in an old folks home one day."

"I would never do that to you. Besides, I'm sure if I ever did take you to an old folk's home, by the end of the day they'd call me to come and get you. They'd be shouting, 'She's insane! She's insane!' And I'd be shouting, 'I know! I know! That's why she's here!'"

The two of them stood silently for a few seconds, then Eleanor asked, "How about Davenport?"

Vegas stared at her mother for a few seconds, then said, "Well, I've enjoyed standing out here talking to you about cars and housekeepers and being a part of your parking instruction course, but I've got an appointment to keep. You wait out here and try and come up with car names better than Davenport."

"Why can't I go in?" Eleanor asked as she grabbed Vegas by the shoulder.

"That's simple, Mom, because I'm talking with a client, not my first-grade teacher."

"But I drove you down here," Eleanor said in a matter-of-fact way.

"You didn't park that well, so that means you have to stay outside. Listen, I wanted to drive myself down here and you wouldn't let me."

"That's because it's my vehicle, which is paid for, by the way. The government won't be coming to take away Bonnie."

"You're going with Bonnie?"

"I think it fits. Well, for now it fits. I'll probably change it again later."

"Why don't you go shopping or something?"

Eleanor smiled enthusiastically. "I can do that. I'll see you in a half-hour or so. I have to make a phone call first."

"Who are you going to call?"

Eleanor began looking in her purse for her phone. "You don't have to know everything that I do. Now you go on ahead." Eleanor then stopped and looked at her daughter. "What was I looking for again?"

"You said your phone."

"You're right," Eleanor said and rummaged some more. "I found it."

"I'm proud of you. I'll try and get a petition to have a statue of you and Bonnie put up on this very spot," Vegas said and headed to the cafe.

Vegas walked in and didn't see anybody but a teenage boy behind the counter scrolling on his phone. Small tables with booth seating lined both sides of the cafe walls, with each table having a roll of paper towels in the center, along with pig salt and pepper shaker figurines. It was very warm inside. Obviously the air conditioner hadn't worked since the 1970s, Vegas thought. Behind the counter was an open window through which the kitchen could be seen. A woman stood over a grill frying something while swinging a flyswatter madly with her right hand. Vegas then heard the men's room door open and out walked a gentleman in a suit carrying a black briefcase.

Vegas asked him, "Excuse me, are you Mr. Harper?"

"Yes. Are you Vegas Chantly?"

"Yes."

"And who's she?"

"What?" asked Vegas, whipping around.

"I'm Eleanor Chantly. I'm my daughter's mother."

Eleanor went to shake hands with Mr. Harper, but Vegas grabbed her by the arm and turned her around, then glanced back at Mr. Harper as she walked away. "Excuse us for a second."

Vegas escorted her mother to a table by the window and whispered, "What are you doing in here?"

"Baby, Mommy's helping. He's kind of handsome isn't he?"

"You're not helping. I thought you had to make a phone call."

"I made it. Things are so easy with a cellphone. You really need to get one."

"I hate computers and technology just like dad did. Now I'm a grown woman that has to get through life by herself. You have to let go of me."

"I'll let go of you after the meeting. I promise. Now let's just go talk things through with that man. You won't even know I'm here. It'll be like I'm invisible."

Eleanor placed her hand on the table beside her and accidentally knocked a roll of paper towels to the floor, where it unrolled itself. She quickly stopped it and began rolling it back up haphazardly, then put it back on the table but hit the lip of the table, knocking the roll out of her hand and sending it across the floor to Mr. Harper's feet. Mr. Harper picked it up and handed it to Eleanor.

"It's almost alive, isn't it?" asked Eleanor with a hardy laugh. "Thank you." Eleanor placed the roll back onto the table.

Vegas stared hard at her mother and whispered, "I know you're here."

Vegas walked to Mr. Harper, who invited them to sit in a booth by the window. Mr. Harper sat on one side, and Vegas and her invisible mother sat on the other.

"Thank you for meeting me on such short notice."

"Not a problem," said Vegas. "What is it that you need me to do?"

"I own a publishing company in New York City called Read a Book Publishers. We're about to be bought out by a larger company–"

"Ca-ching!" Eleanor said and moved her index finger down in the air as if she was pushing a key on a cash register.

"Mom, your invisibility is wearing off," Vegas whispered through gritted teeth. Eleanor mimed zipping her mouth shut and then began to play with the pig salt shaker.

"Well, our biggest seller is our Riddles and Riches puzzle."

"Puzzle?" quizzed Vegas. "You mean like a jigsaw puzzle or a word puzzle?"

"It's sort of like a jigsaw puzzle, but there aren't any interlocking pieces. Here, I brought one with me."

Mr. Harper picked up his briefcase, placed it on the table, and opened it. He took out a box that was roughly nine inches by twelve inches and about two inches thick. Before he closed the briefcase, Vegas saw a brochure for a casino in Bristol, Virginia. Mr. Harper then set the box in the middle of the table and placed his briefcase back on the floor.

"This is the puzzle," said Mr. Harper. "It's by far our best-selling item."

"Oh, I love puzzles," said Eleanor. "I'm always putting one together after supper. It helps me relax. I'm doing one with a clown and a dog now. Do you own a dog?"

Mr. Harper looked bemused. "No. I don't own a dog – or a clown, for that matter."

Vegas whispered to her mother, "Maybe you should go home now and work on your puzzle."

"Sorry," Eleanor said and fiddled with the pig salt shaker again.

Vegas looked at the puzzle box. "There's no image of the puzzle on the box."

"That's the beauty of it," said Mr. Harper. "Nobody knows what the puzzle image is supposed to be."

"Then why would anybody buy it?" asked Vegas.

"Because when you get the puzzle put together, you will find some sort of clue that leads to a treasure. That's why it's called Riddles and Riches."

"Do you know what the puzzle is?" asked Vegas.

"No. This was designed by Walter Peabody, one of my employees. Well, former employee. Nobody knows where he is now."

Eleanor dropped the pig salt shaker, and it landed under the table with a clatter. Eleanor said nothing as she slid down under the table to retrieve it. As she attempted to get back up, she bumped her head on the underside of the table several times before she finally was able to take her seat. Vegas took the salt shaker from her mother and placed it back in the center of the table.

"What exactly is it that you want me to do?" Vegas asked Mr. Harper.

"I want you to put the puzzle together and find the treasure."

"You don't know where the treasure is?" asked Vegas.

"No. However, Mr. Peabody was originally from Georgia, so there are rumors that it could be in the state somewhere."

Eleanor said, "I lose things all the time, but when I finally find them, they're like little treasures to me. I once lost the TV remote control, and my neighbor found it in their freezer. I went over there one day and they gave me some ice cream, but for the life of me I don't know why I took the TV remote. But when I got it back it was like a treasure to me. A cold treasure." She laughed but quickly stopped when she saw her daughter's pained expression.

Vegas asked, "Since you're the owner of the company, how come you didn't require this Walter Peabody to tell you where the treasure was before you made the puzzle?"

"He's one of my best employees. The most trustworthy."

"That's all fine and good, but I would think it would be best to know where the treasure was before you made the puzzle."

"Well, he supplied the treasure for the puzzle."

"He did?" asked Vegas.

"It's just like I'm your treasure," Eleanor said to her daughter. "I supplied myself to be your treasure and you are so welcome." Eleanor then added a kiss on her daughter's cheek for emphasis.

Vegas whispered through her gritted teeth, "I thought you said I wouldn't even know you were here."

"I thought adding some wit to the conversation would help," Eleanor whispered.

"I really wish you'd do something else besides talk."

"I was until you took my salt shaker away."

Vegas closed her eyes and counted to ten quietly. She

composed herself and asked Mr. Harper, "Do you know what the treasure is?"

"Oh, yes. It's gold and silver coins. There are one hundred one-ounce gold coins and one thousand silver coins. There's also a fifty-ounce gold bar. He also has some old baseball cards. Rookie cards of Hall of Famers like Babe Ruth, Lou Gehrig, Joe DiMaggio, Mickey Mantle, Ty Cobb. It's very valuable."

"And he supplied all of this?" Vegas asked with wonder.

"Yes. See, he inherited the gold and silver, and he bought the baseball cards. He never married and didn't have any family that he was close to, so he asked me if he could make a treasure and a puzzle. I thought it was a great idea."

"Did he get any royalties from the puzzle?" asked Vegas.

"Oh, yes, seventy percent."

"That's a generous royalty."

"Well, he supplied the treasure, designed the puzzle and all of the clues, then buried the treasure. But then we lost contact with him, and we haven't been able to pay him the royalties. They're in an account waiting for him if we ever find him."

Vegas drank in all the information Mr. Harper was giving her. "The clues are on the puzzle?"

"Yes. That's how he told me he designed it. When you get the puzzle together, that is your first clue. It shows you where to go. Then from there you find another clue, which takes you to another clue. There are five clues from puzzle to treasure. It's been selling like hotcakes."

"Where did that saying come from?" asked Eleanor.

"I'm not sure," said Mr. Harper.

"Is a hotcake the same as a pancake?"

"I'm not sure," said Mr. Harper.

"Do you all want me to Google it?" Eleanor asked as she grabbed her purse to look for her cellphone.

"Mom, please," Vegas said and began rubbing her forehead with her left hand.

"I was just trying to help Mr. Harper learn," said Eleanor in a defensive tone. "You know, pancakes always filled me up. They set heavy on my chest. I feel full for the rest of the day, and all I want to do is lie down and sleep. I like bacon, though. It makes me smile. That's probably why I like this pig salt shaker so much. How do you spell Google?"

"Mom, can't you go wait outside until Mr. Harper and I finish talking?"

"It's okay," said Mr. Harper in a reassuring tone. "I have a mother that embarrasses me, too."

"I don't think I embarrass anybody," said Eleanor defensively.

"Okay, help then," Mr. Harper said with a smile.

"I do that all right," said a grinning Eleanor.

"Let's get back to the case here," Vegas said. "So you want me to put this puzzle together and follow the clues until I find the treasure?"

"That's correct."

"When I find the treasure, what do you want me to do?"

"Just take a photograph of it and each clue and give me all the coordinates, then I'll give it to the company that wants to buy me out. I need to reassure them that the treasure exists."

Vegas thought it over for a few seconds. "I can do that."

"A treasure hunt sounds like fun," Eleanor said as she rubbed her hands together.

Vegas pulled out her business card from her front pants pocket and handed it to Mr. Harper. "This is my card, and my rates are on the back. Are you okay with that?"

Mr. Harper flipped the card over and read the rates and smiled. "That's fine. I really need to find this treasure so the deal can go through." He stood up. "Now, I really need to get back to New York."

Vegas and Eleanor stood, and they shook hands with Mr. Harper. Then Mr. Harper gave Vegas his business card. "Call my cellphone any time, day or night, to let me know how things are going."

"I'll do that," said Vegas.

"I look forward to hearing from you," said Mr. Harper as he left.

Vegas held the puzzle box in her hand and stared at it.

"Now what?" asked Eleanor.

"We put together this puzzle."

"When I was little, I had a puzzle of two clowns. I used to put it together all the time until I dropped it in the commode."

"Why did you have your puzzle in the bathroom?"

"Who knows?"

"I'll keep the puzzle at my house."

"You mean camper."

"It still counts."

"Vegas ..." said Eleanor as she began feeling her right rear pant leg.

"What?"

"I think I sat on some gum."

Vegas turned her mother around and saw the wad of gum stuck to her mother's pants.

"Hold still and I'll get it off."

CHAPTER 3

ELEANOR DROVE while Vegas sat in the passenger's seat thinking about the case and looking at the puzzle box in her lap.

"I was very proud of you back there," Eleanor said with pride. "The way you conducted yourself like a professional was very rewarding."

Vegas sighed. "It's kind of hard to act professional when your mother is under the table."

"Well, accidents happen," Eleanor reasoned.

"You could have loaned me your vehicle and avoided any accidents."

"There's no fun in that. It's good for us to have mother-daughter time. It makes for a healthy relationship. Don't you think?"

"You don't want to know what I think about our mother-daughter time," Vegas said as she opened the puzzle box and looked inside.

"When was the last time you worked a jigsaw puzzle?" asked Eleanor.

"It's been awhile, I guess. But this is the first time I opened a jigsaw puzzle that doesn't have any interlocking pieces.

There must be thousands of tiny puzzle pieces here," Vegas said, scooping up a handful of pieces. "All the pieces are white on one side and red on the other with lines running across them on both sides. Which side is the image with the clue?"

"We will figure it out."

"Maybe it's a combination of the two sides– Wait, what do you mean by we will figure it out?"

"I'm a jigsaw puzzle champion. Don't you remember me telling you back at the cafe?"

"I've been trying to block out everything you did back there. Anyway, this is a very complicated puzzle."

"You need to relax," suggested Eleanor. "When I need to relax I watch soccer."

"Soccer?" Vegas asked in a confused voice. "You don't even like sports."

"I know. But when I watch soccer, I fall asleep. It's better than any over-the-counter sleep aid."

Vegas noticed that her mother was making her way toward the bank drive-thru. "Why are you going to the bank?"

"I need to withdraw some funds, you know, just to pay some bills is all. It's nothing more than that. A woman needs to pay her bills. You don't want mommy to go to jail, do you?"

"Mom, you're acting very strange. Stranger than usual – and that is saying something. Are you about to rob the place?"

"I'm not going to rob the bank," Eleanor said with a nervous laugh. "You know, something just occurred to me."

"Here we go," Vegas said under her breath.

"If money doesn't grow on trees, then why are banks called branches?"

"I don't know, Mom."

"It's amazing the things a body can think of while waiting in line at the bank drive-thru. Somebody should look into that."

The car crept closer to the drive-thru window, and Eleanor pulled a withdrawal slip from her purse and filled it in as Vegas concentrated on the puzzle.

"I think it's very odd that Mr. Harper didn't check out the location of the clues," said Vegas. "That doesn't make any sense whatsoever. No one is that trusting of somebody else, especially of an employee. He could have at least made him write down where the clues were."

"I trust you, sweetie. I wouldn't ask you to tell me where the clues were. I know you would do your best because you are so wonderful."

"That's a little thick, Mom," said Vegas, her suspicions growing over her mother's actions. Eleanor pulled up to the teller window.

"Hello," the female teller said happily.

"Hello," replied Eleanor. "How are you?"

"I'm fine. How can I help you?"

"You can find my daughter a husband," Eleanor said with a chuckle.

"Mom!" shouted Vegas, who then propped her elbow on the side of the passenger door and buried her face into her hand.

"I need to withdraw some money from my account." Eleanor went to drop the slip into the drawer but missed. "Oh, shoot. I missed the bucket."

"It's a drawer, Mom."

Eleanor tried to open her door to retrieve the withdrawal slip, but she was too close to the bank and couldn't open the door. "I'm stuck. Vegas, Mommy's stuck. Can you get out and get my withdrawal slip?"

Vegas opened her door while muttering, "How can you miss a bucket, I mean drawer?" Vegas walked around to the front of the vehicle, but didn't see the slip. "Where's it at?"

Eleanor stuck her head out of the window. "Maybe it went under the vehicle."

"I can't believe this day right now," Vegas said as she knelt down and peered under the vehicle and saw the slip. She got down onto her stomach, reached out, and grabbed the withdrawal slip, then stood up and put it in the bank drawer. She looked at the bank window lady and told her, "Now you'll have something to put in your company newsletter."

Vegas got back in her seat and saw her mother watching her. She was about to ask again why she was acting so strangely when it hit her.

"Mom, that phone call you had to make outside Reno's ..."

"Yes."

"Who was that to?"

Eleanor appeared to be trying to think of something to say. "It was just an old friend that I used to know back in high school. I sent him an email."

"What old friend?"

"Pepper," Eleanor said, and immediately got mad at herself. "I wasn't supposed to say that. I mean Wilson Culpepper."

"Why would you call my friend Pepper? You don't even like him. You think he looks like a homeless monster."

"I said Pepper by mistake. I meant Culpepper. They're both condiments, so it's easy to get them mixed up. I think they're condiments. Is Culpepper a condiment or a vegetable? I always get those two confused."

"Are you trying to buy the vehicle from Pepper for me?"

"No. I wouldn't do that."

The teller opened the bank drawer and said, "Here's your money. Thank you."

"Thank you," said Eleanor as she attempted to reach from the height of her SUV down into the drawer to retrieve the cash. "I can't get a good grasp on it. Vegas, hold Mommy's feet."

"What?"

"Hold my feet so I don't tumble out. You don't want your mother to tumble out of the window, do you? Then you'd have to crawl under the vehicle again and get me out from under it."

Vegas watched in horror as her mother undid her seatbelt and hung her body out the window. She looked like a fat cat trying to fit through a small cat door, Vegas thought. Being the dutiful daughter, Vegas quickly grabbed her mother's feet so she wouldn't fall out.

Eleanor shouted, "I got it! I knew I could get it. I just had to get into the right position is all. Those exercises I've been doing are working. Jumping jacks must be giving me length. But they aren't helping my memory any because I usually forget to do them."

"Mom, I don't want your money or the memory of most of this day."

Eleanor shook her head. "I don't understand you. They say once your child gets to be a teenager, they think they know everything."

"I'm not a child. I'm a grown woman holding my mother's feet at the bank."

"Well, you have to have a vehicle. You can't afford to get one yourself, so it's up to me to help. It's okay, that's what mothers are supposed to do."

"But you don't have to buy it for me. I can do that myself."

"I wanted to buy that red car for you, but you said, 'No, Mom, I can buy it all by myself, I'm a grownup lady now,' and you had to give it back."

"I didn't say I was a grownup lady," Vegas said as she looked in the side mirror and saw the man in the car behind them throw up his hands in exasperation.

"Well, I remember differently," said Eleanor. "You didn't let me help you and you had to give the car back. Am I right?"

Vegas sat in her seat stewing.

The woman at the drive-thru window said, "Uh ... you all are holding up the line."

"Oh, I'm sorry," said Eleanor. "I was giving a financial lesson to my daughter. She's smart in a lot of things, just not in the financials. She's a private investigator, by the way. If you think your man is cheating on you, she can help." Eleanor turned to her daughter. "Do you have a business card I can give her? She's having husband issues."

"I'm not married, ma'am," said the bank teller.

"Mom, leave her alone so we can go."

Eleanor turned back to the bank teller. "I'll see you later. Oh, what was your name?"

"Karoline."

"Thanks, Karoline. You wouldn't have a job for my daughter, would you?"

"Mom, I have a job."

"I bet Karoline could afford a Volkswagen."

"Can we just go before the people behind us start throwing rocks at us to get us to move?"

"Okay," Eleanor said as she waved at Karoline and sat up straight in her seat to see better. "Make sure Mommy doesn't hit that pillar on your side. I always get nervous driving through here. I'm afraid I'm going to hit the pillar and the roof will fall down on me and, well, I'd be killed by the roof at the bank drive-thru. Honey, if that happens, please move into my house and sell that camper, but tell everybody I died some other way."

"Yes, mother."

CHAPTER 4

ELEANOR PARKED in front of her daughter's camper at the Pine Sap campsite a little after one o'clock. Vegas was staring so intently at the puzzle in her lap, she didn't notice they were at her home.

"I wonder how many people have tried solving this puzzle," Vegas wondered aloud. "And if they haven't done it, then how in the world am I going to do it?"

"Because you've got the brains of your father and the looks of your mother," Eleanor said.

Vegas looked at her mother. "How are the looks of my mother going to help me solve a puzzle?"

"It'll make you look good doing it."

A yellow Volkswagen parked behind Eleanor's SUV. Vegas and Eleanor got out of the SUV and watched as Pepper eased his hulking frame out of the tiny yellow vehicle, looking like a snake trying to shed its skin. He sighed when he was clear of the car, and looked at Vegas and Eleanor.

"I know what a can of wieners feels like now," he said as he stretched out by attempting to touch his toes.

"Is this the vehicle you were telling me about?" asked Vegas.

"This is it," Pepper said as he stretched his long arms above his head. "I traded a box of comic books for it."

"Comic books?" asked Eleanor. "Well, I have to admit it does look like Tweety Bird. There's more yellow in that Volkswagen than there is in the sun."

Vegas handed the puzzle box to her mother. "Hold this for a second and don't lose it."

"I'm not going to lose it," said Eleanor. But before she even got the sentence out of her mouth, she dropped the box. She quickly scooped it up. "Found it!"

Vegas ignored her mother, then opened the door to the Volkswagen and looked inside. "It's a manual shift."

"Yeah, that's how they made Volkswagens back in 1962."

"It's been a long time since I drove a manual," said Vegas as she sat in the driver's seat and began to feel around the vehicle.

"I'm sure it'll come back to you," Eleanor said before turning to Pepper. "Her father taught her how to drive a manual, or the big stick, as the young people call it. He tried to teach me, too, but his screaming in fear kind of got on my nerves, so I had to stop."

"Give it a drive and see what you think," suggested Pepper. "The keys are in the ignition."

"Okay," Vegas said as she enthusiastically closed the door.

"I want to come with you," Eleanor said as she hurried around to the passenger's side door and got in with the puzzle box.

"What do you think?" asked Vegas through her beaming smile.

"It's fine," said Eleanor. "But what you think about it is more important than what I think. Do you like it?"

"I think I actually love it."

"Then I love it, too. This Volkswagen can be my grandchild until you get on the ball."

Vegas ignored her mother's comment and started the engine. "It sounds fine."

Pepper squatted down and stuck his large head through the driver's side window. "I went all through the engine. It runs great."

"Does it have air conditioning?" asked Vegas.

"No."

"A heater?" asked Eleanor.

"It does have a heater, but when you turn it on, the right headlight goes out."

"Why does it do that?" asked Eleanor.

"It wants to," replied Pepper.

"Does it have any other quirks that I should know about?" asked Vegas.

"The engine is in the back."

"It has two engines?" asked Eleanor as she looked toward the back.

"No, Mom, it only has one engine, and it's in the back of the car instead of the front."

"That's strange," said Eleanor. "Is the glove compartment in the back, too? Oh, no, here it is," Eleanor added as she opened the glove box in front of her.

"We'll be right back," Vegas told Pepper as she put the gear into reverse, eased out the clutch to back up, then stopped, put it into first and drove off. Eleanor gave out a happy "Yahoo!" as Vegas drove down the gravel road toward the camper park exit.

"It seems to drive well," observed Eleanor.

"I like it. I just need to get used to driving a manual. The last manual I drove was that blue Chevy truck Dad had."

"I hated that truck. I had to move it one time while he was out of town so I could get my vehicle out, and I couldn't get the stupid thing moved because I kept killing the engine."

"So what did you do?"

"I called a taxi and had him move it. Do you know he charged me twenty bucks just to move that truck?"

"You're doing wonders for the women's movement."

"Hey, I solved the situation. That's all that matters. A woman has to get her hair done."

Vegas turned the Volkswagen around and headed back to her camper, where they found Pepper stretching against the camper.

"Are you trying to push my camper over?" asked Vegas as she got out. Her home moved slightly as he pushed against it.

"No. I'm still feeling cramped. That was a tight fit."

"How many tries did it take you to squeeze in that tiny thing anyway?" asked Vegas.

"Six. Me and the steering wheel are now engaged."

"At least you're seeing someone," said Eleanor as she glared at her dateless daughter.

Vegas ignored her mother and said, "I'll take it."

"Great," said Pepper.

"Here's your money," said Eleanor as she handed Pepper the envelope of cash she got from the bank.

"Thanks."

"Oh, no you don't," Vegas said as she attempted to grab the envelope.

"Put it above your head!" shouted Eleanor, which a confused Pepper did.

"I'll pay for my own vehicle," Vegas said as she tried to get the envelope out of Pepper's hands.

"I'll pay for your vehicle, and you can pay me back by hanging out with me more," suggested Eleanor.

Vegas stopped jumping. "More? You're at my door every morning."

"I have to see what you need."

"My arm is getting tired," said Pepper.

Vegas reached into her pocket and began digging around. "Does that envelope have a fifty in it?"

"I don't know," replied Pepper. "You all made me put it above my head before I had a chance to look inside it."

"Well, look and see," demanded Vegas.

Pepper looked into the envelope while he held it above his head. He took out a fifty dollar bill. "Here's one."

"I'll give you a fifty and you can give that fifty to my mother so at least I'm paying something on my vehicle," instructed Vegas as she kept searching her pockets for cash.

"If that makes you feel any better, then that's what we'll do," said Eleanor.

Vegas finally found a bill in her shirt pocket. It was a ten. "Does that envelope have a ten dollar bill in it?"

"Do I put the fifty back?" asked Pepper.

"Yeah," Vegas said gloomily.

Pepper looked up into his envelope that he was still holding above his head. "I don't see a ten dollar bill in it. Listen, if you need some money, I can loan you some."

"I don't need money," argued Vegas. "All I need is my pride."

"Good luck paying your bills with pride," mumbled Eleanor.

"Here, take this ten dollar bill and add it to the total," said Vegas as she handed the money to Pepper.

"I'm afraid to put my hands down because I might get into trouble," said Pepper.

"I have a ten," said Eleanor as she put it in Pepper's pocket. "Now we're all even out."

"How are we evened out?" asked Vegas.

"I paid the ten dollars for your vehicle."

"Now you're ten dollars ahead of me," said Vegas.

"You all don't owe me ten more dollars," said Pepper.

"Give me the ten," said Vegas.

"Can I let my hands down?"

"Yes!" shouted Vegas.

Pepper slowly let his hands down and took the ten dollar bill from his pocket. Vegas grabbed it and handed him her ten dollar bill, then took the ten dollar bill her mother gave Pepper and handed it back to Eleanor.

"Now you take this," demanded Vegas.

"No," Eleanor said, and began running around the yard with Vegas chasing her, demanding that she take her ten dollar bill back.

"What the heck is going on here?" Vegas could hear Pepper ask nobody in particular.

CHAPTER 5

THE SUN STOOD high in the sky when Vegas and Eleanor ended their chase and entered the camper breathing heavily.

"I can't believe you chased your mother all over the yard," Eleanor said as she collapsed on the bed.

"I had to prove my worth to you," Vegas said as she reached into her tiny refrigerator and pulled out a bottle of water, then proceeded to drink half of it in one go. "Do you want something to drink?"

Eleanor simply lifted her arm, as if she was too tired to even speak. Vegas got another bottle of water and gave it to Eleanor. She sat up and took a big drink.

"Ah! That's good water," Eleanor said. "Where did you get it?"

"I got it at Bernie's – you know, the store on the corner of Franklin and Willow. I think it's called Bernie's. It's where I usually get gas. They're the only place that sells this brand of water. I think it's good."

Eleanor looked at the label. "Wett Water. That's an interesting name."

"Apparently the guy that started it has the last name of Wett."

"Where do they get the water from?"

"Probably from the bathroom sink at their house."

Pepper poked his head in the door. "Are you two okay?"

"We're fine," said Vegas. "Thanks for not calling the cops on us."

"I know not to come between money negotiations of a mother and daughter. Besides, I wouldn't have called the cops. I would have probably called the mental health agency. You all forgot your puzzle out here, by the way," said Pepper. Vegas snatched it out of his hand.

"Mom, did you drop this outside?" Vegas asked incredulously.

Eleanor chugged the rest of the bathroom sink water, wiped her mouth, and stared at Vegas. "I guess I did. In my defense, I was being chased by a mad woman. I got so tired that I had to ditch weight. My pants were going to be the next thing to go."

"I'm glad our chase ended at the big rock."

"I didn't know you were into puzzles," said Pepper.

"It's for my next case."

"Were you hired by a kindergarten teacher or something?" asked Pepper.

"No," said Vegas defensively. "It's for a publishing company. Nobody has been able to put the puzzle together, and they want me to put it together and follow the clues that lead to a treasure."

"Hey, I think I've heard of that," Pepper said and stepped into the camper, which caused it to dip down. He took the box back and began examining it. Eleanor joined the group, and the three of them stood together like subway passengers heading to Yonkers.

"Wait," said Vegas. "We need to go outside to the picnic table and look at this. It's too crowded in here."

"I feel like I'm still in the Volkswagen," said Pepper.

"You're going to be through my floor if we don't get out of here," said Vegas.

"If you'd buy a real house, you wouldn't have this problem," pointed out Eleanor. "Shoot, if you bought a box, you wouldn't have this problem."

The three of them went outside and sat at the picnic table near the camper, Vegas and Eleanor on one side, and Pepper on the other. Vegas opened the box and emptied the contents onto the table.

Pepper picked up the lid of the box. "There's no picture on the box. How do you know what you're putting together if there's no picture on it?"

"I guess they don't want it to be too easy," said Eleanor as she took the lid and looked at it.

"I don't see any instructions," observed Vegas as she searched through the square pieces of the puzzle.

"Why would you need instructions?" asked Eleanor. "Everybody knows how to put together a jigsaw puzzle."

"But it's supposed to be riddles and treasure. Seems like they would have something in here about that," Vegas said as she took the box cover from her mother. "It doesn't seem to play it up very well on the outside of the box, either. All it says is, 'Inside the lid is the first clue to your treasure.'"

"Some of the images are peeling off," Pepper said as he examined a piece.

"This seems pretty shoddy, doesn't it?" asked Vegas. "You'd think it would be better made than this since it's supposed to lead to a treasure."

"Maybe they do it like that so you can't solve it," said Pepper.

"This piece doesn't look as square as the other pieces," said

Eleanor. "It's shaped like a walrus. Don't you think it looks like a walrus?"

"No," Vegas said.

"What about you, Pepper? Do you think it looks like a walrus?"

Pepper stared at the puzzle piece in question. "I might think that after a few beers."

"I think it looks like a walrus."

"What is this image supposed to be of, anyway?" asked Pepper.

"It would be funny if it was a walrus," said Eleanor with a laugh. "That would teach you two."

"It's supposed to give you clues to where the treasure is, but it doesn't tell you what the image is, so you have to figure it out on your own," said Vegas.

"That's interesting," said Pepper. "A puzzle within a puzzle so you don't know what it's supposed to be. I'm impressed. But there's no image on the pieces, just red on one side and white on the other with lines. Is it a map?"

"I don't know. The workmanship is so terrible, too," added Vegas. "It doesn't even look like something they would allow on the marketplace, because it would make them look bad."

"All anybody is going to worry about is the treasure," said Pepper. "They don't care about the quality of the puzzle. Just that it gives them their clue."

"It just doesn't seem to fit into my mind," observed Vegas.

"Where did you buy it?" asked Pepper.

Eleanor interjected, "The handsome publisher man gave it to me."

"Me," corrected Vegas. "He gave it to me. You were busy not being invisible."

"He gave it to us. I was there being encouraging."

"The publishing company hired you two to put a puzzle together?" asked Pepper.

"They hired one of us," Vegas said.

"It was buy one, get one free," Eleanor said with a hearty laugh.

Vegas rolled her eyes.

"Shouldn't the puzzle company know all of this before they put out the puzzle?" asked Pepper.

"The guy trusted Walter Peabody with the project," Vegas said.

"Walter Peabody?" mused Pepper. "Was he that dog in the old *Bullwinkle* cartoon?"

"No, that was *Mr.* Peabody," Vegas said. "I don't even know if he had a first name."

"I remember you used to watch that as a kid," reminisced Eleanor. "You were afraid of the flying squirrel on the show."

"Why were you afraid of Rocky?" asked Pepper. "I thought he showed wonderful skills as an actor."

"I wasn't afraid of Rocky," Vegas said defensively.

"Who's Rocky?" asked Eleanor.

"The flying squirrel," Vegas said with a sigh.

"That's an odd name for a squirrel," said Eleanor. "They should have called him Nutty or Mr. Tail. Well, anyway, Vegas would sit in the middle of the floor drinking her hot chocolate watching the show. She would get real gassy from the hot chocolate, too. Do you remember that? She stunk up the whole house. I finally had to make her drink it out on the porch."

"Can we leave my childhood alone for a while?"

"Why were you afraid of Rocky?" asked a concerned Pepper.

"I don't know. I was just a kid, for crying out loud. A kid with childhood trauma issues and gas." Vegas turned her attention back to the puzzle. "This doesn't seem to be making an image at all – none of the lines match up."

"Is something missing?" Pepper asked.

"We just opened the box," said Vegas. "And we got it from the publisher himself. You know, maybe there's a faint image on the puzzle instead of a clear one. Some sort of optical illusion where you have to look at it a certain way to figure it out."

"This sounds very James Bondish," observed Eleanor. "But which side of the pieces is the correct side?" She flipped over a puzzle piece in her hand.

"I'm guessing it has to be a combination of both sides," said Vegas. "It wants to frustrate and confuse you so you can't put it together, so then you can't get the treasure. After all, the longer the treasure goes unclaimed, the more puzzles they can sell and the more money they can make."

The three of them spent the rest of the day trying different ways to establish some sort of pattern on the puzzle, but nothing came of their efforts.

"This is impossible," said Eleanor. "It's like trying to find something good to watch on television."

"You should check out *Ancient Aliens* on the History Channel," suggested Pepper. "I love that show."

"I've never heard of it," said Eleanor.

"They talk about aliens from outer space and–"

Eleanor interrupted Pepper. "I mean I've never heard of the History Channel."

"Let's concentrate, people," interrupted Vegas. "It seems like we're missing something. This just isn't making sense."

"If we could figure it out in a day, someone else would have, too," said Pepper.

"How would you know if someone found the treasure?" asked Eleanor.

"You would call it in or something?" Vegas suggested. "But

there's nothing on the box that says what to do. It all seems incomplete to me."

Pepper stood up and stretched his long arms above his head and let out a groan that sounded like a bull bumping into a barn door.

"Do you need a ride home?" Vegas asked Pepper.

"Nah, I called Big Shelly to come get me."

"Wait, called?" asked Vegas. "I thought you refused to get a phone because the government would use it to spy on you."

"I made one that can't be tracked."

"Made one?" asked Vegas. "Is that legal?"

"If the government wanted us to be obedient, then they shouldn't have funded the internet."

"Fair enough, I guess. Who is Big Shelly?" asked Vegas.

"Is she your girlfriend?" Eleanor asked with a grin.

"No," replied Pepper with an embarrassed smile. "I'm not in her league. We're going to go Wood Booger hunting tonight in the Sloppy Swamp."

"Wood Booger hunting?" asked Vegas and Eleanor simultaneously.

"It's what they call Bigfoot in the Appalachian Mountains," informed Pepper. "So that's what we call our society, The Wood Booger Society. We're all going looking for them the next few days, and some are even going to camp out. We thought if everyone was out looking for them at the same time, we'd be more likely to find them."

"There's a Wood Booger in Sloppy Swamp?" asked Eleanor.

"Oh, yeah, it's been seen by several people. There's a video of it on YouTube. Of course, it looks more like a large stump in the distance at first, but then it moves. It's fantastic. It's the greatest evidence ever of a Wood Booger. I'm sure the guy that filmed it wouldn't lie."

"I'm sure he wouldn't," Vegas said in an unsure voice.

A Toyota pickup truck pulled up, and a short, egg-shaped woman who resembled Humpty Dumpty's little sister got out and walked to them. She was wearing a flannel shirt, jeans and a baseball cap with the catchy slogan "My Hat" blazoned across the front of it in plaid colors.

"Did you have any trouble finding the place?" asked Pepper.

"No, I just followed your scent."

"Great. Oh, this is Big Shelly."

"I'm honored to meet you people," Big Shelly said as she sternly shook Vegas' and Eleanor's hands.

"Well, I guess we'll be heading out," said Pepper. "We need to get into the woods before it gets dark. That's when Wood Boogers like to roam."

"I've been practicing my Wood Booger howl," said Big Shelly.

Before anybody could say, "please don't," Big Shelly cupped her right hand to the side of her mouth and bellowed out a deep scream that sounded like half bear and half mental patient combined into one problem. Big Shelly did it three times, and even Pepper was becoming uncomfortable.

"That's really... uh, different," Eleanor complimented before she said the phrase that Vegas feared the most. "Let me try it."

Vegas quickly pulled her mother back down as she began to stand for the clearest of bellows. "We don't want you to call out a Wood Booger, Mom. Remember, you're not a professional like Big Shelly here. Something bad might happen."

"We should go hunting for the Wood Booger one night," suggested Eleanor. "It would be good bonding time between mother and daughter."

"No, Mom, it would not be a good anything between mother and daughter."

Pepper said, "You don't technically have to look for a Wood Booger in the dark. We have several trail cameras set up, and we'll review them, too. You all could try something like that."

"We're good," said Vegas.

"I think it would be good for us to go out Wood Booger hunting," added Eleanor. "Maybe we could go with you two?"

"No, Mom, I'm working, remember?"

"Oh, well, when it comes to going on vacation, we have a plan of action," Eleanor said with a chuckle. "Wood Booger, here we come! I'll practice my Wood Booger calls in the shower."

"You shouldn't be scaring the neighbors, Mom."

"I already do that."

"Well, we'll see you all around. Hope you get the puzzle figured out," said Pepper.

"We will," Eleanor shouted emphatically.

Pepper and Big Shelly got in the truck and drove off. Vegas turned back to the puzzle and stared at it, depressed.

"Do you think the two of them will get married?" Eleanor asked.

"They're just going out looking for Wood Boogers. It's not a date, Mom."

"Dates can take any shape. If you can date a person on a computer, you can date them while in the woods looking for a Wood Booger."

"I just don't understand how this puzzle works."

"It's meant to be complicated, Vegas. You don't want everybody finding the treasure."

"It just seems like something is missing. I don't know what it is, but something doesn't seem right here."

"You need a break. Want to go to the Dixie Discount before they close? I have to get a lamp. I knocked one over with the vacuum cleaner yesterday. I got the vacuum cord wrapped around the lamp cord, and it toppled right over and broke. I loved that lamp, too. I bought it from a Fingerhut catalog years ago."

"Maybe a break would do me good. No pun intended. We can take the Volkswagen."

"Sure. You can practice driving it and getting to know all its features."

"Let's go then," Vegas said as she gathered up the puzzle and put the box inside the camper.

"This is going to be a great little adventure," Eleanor said.

"It's just us going to buy a lamp."

"But you never know what's going to happen when you head out. Well, I know we're going to the Dixie Discount, but other than that, anything can happen."

CHAPTER 6

VEGAS PULLED the yellow Volkswagen over in front of the Dixie Discount at the Atta Boy Mini Mall in downtown Falls Branch, Georgia.

"I am loving this little yellow bug," said Eleanor.

"Yeah, but I just wish that I could get the hang of pulling out better. When I drift backward, it fills me with anxiety. If I have to pull out on a hill, I may have some trouble – especially if a car is behind me."

"All it takes is practice. I can help you."

"How will you do that?"

"By always being by your side and shouting encouragement," Eleanor said and shouted in a deep voice: "Forward ho, backward ho, whichever one is relevant for the moment."

Vegas rolled her eyes as they walked toward the entrance of the store. Eleanor recollected, "I saw on YouTube that a woman was talking about her mother and said she was a godsend for helping her. What is it like having me help you?"

"It's like putting me in a big balloon and shaking me real hard."

"I'm going to interpret that as 'fun.'"

The two of them walked into the Dixie Discount and began

looking about. The store had a wide variety of items, from toys and clothes to household goods. All the aisles were close together, and there were shelves full of merchandise that went all the way to the ceiling. Unopened boxes of goods were stacked in the aisles, making it hard to walk about.

"They have so much stuff here," observed Eleanor. "I've come down here before and spent hours just looking around. I bought my Laurel and Hardy tiny statues here. Did I show them to you?"

"No."

"I put them in my curio cabinet in the dining room. I bet they'll be worth a lot of money one day. They were made in Vietnam in the 1990s."

"Careful, I might off you for the giant inheritance they bring," Vegas joked.

"That's why I keep the curio cabinet locked," Eleanor said with a smile.

"Why do they have all of these unopened boxes in the aisles?" asked Vegas.

"They haven't had time to put them up yet."

"But it makes the store all cluttered."

"We all are," said Eleanor.

"Do they have carts?"

"No, they don't have those anymore. They kept them outside, but somebody stole them."

"Somebody stole all of their shopping carts?"

"They must have had a bus for a getaway vehicle."

Eleanor began browsing, and Vegas glanced up at a shelf and saw a puzzle box with the words *The Riddles & Riches Treasure Puzzle*. She stared at it hard for almost a minute. The box was different from the one Davis Harper gave her. The colors were brighter and the lettering sharper. It looked more professional than the one she had.

Vegas looked to her right and saw a step ladder leaned up against the wall with a Bionic Woman action figure without its right leg setting on top of it. She removed it and placed the figure on a nearby shelf next to a wind-up gorilla that played cymbals. Vegas moved the ladder underneath the puzzle and climbed up to retrieve it.

As she was blowing the dust off the box, her mother came down the aisle carrying a lamp covered in painted cats on both the shade and base.

"What did you get?" asked Eleanor.

"The *Riddles & Riches* puzzle."

"You have that at home. You don't know how to shop at all, do you?"

"It looks different. Don't you think it looks different than the one Mr. Harper gave me?"

"Small correction," Eleanor added with a whisper. "He gave it to us. Remember, I was there being invisible."

"I'm trying to forget you were there."

"What does it being different have to do with anything? A puzzle is a puzzle. If you can't get the one worked back at your house, what makes you think you can get this one together?"

"It's a hunch," Vegas said and headed to the front to check out.

"I have those all the time. That's how I found this lamp. I had a hunch it would be in the lamp aisle. It wasn't, though. It was beside a Yogi Bear punching bag. Hunches can be mysterious."

The two checked out, then headed toward their vehicle.

"This little VW of yours stands out," observed Eleanor. "Its shape and color makes it look like a big yellow ball. Hope it doesn't get attacked by a giant cat. Which so happens to be the theme of my lamp!"

"I don't believe there are any giant cats around here, Mom."

"Well, apparently there's a Wood Booger."

"Do you believe that a Wood Booger owns a giant cat?"

"Honey, nobody owns a cat. All they do is tolerate you. They're like the cool kids in school."

Vegas opened the rear of the vehicle but realized after opening it that it was the engine bay.

"I'm going to do that every time," Vegas mumbled as she shook her head.

"Why did they put the engine in the back?"

"To annoy Americans," retorted Vegas.

"Task completed," Eleanor said and made a checkmark in the air.

Vegas and Eleanor walked to the front of the vehicle and opened its trunk, then placed the puzzle in, but the lampshade was too big to fit.

"This small trunk may cause me some issues in the future," observed Vegas.

"We'll need to make sure that your future husband has a bigger trunk than yours. Do you think it'll fit in the backseat?" said Eleanor.

"It might fit back there if we can maneuver it in," replied Vegas. She opened the passenger side door and attempted to lean the front seat forward, but it wouldn't budge.

"What's wrong?" asked Eleanor.

"It's not releasing."

"You have to pull or push a latch or something like that."

"Mom, I know how a front seat is leaned forward."

"Apparently not," whispered Eleanor.

"It's not working and you're not helping," Vegas said as she tried yet again to move the seat.

"I'm not helping because you won't let me. You need to

put some weight into it, and you don't have any. Now let Mommy try. Mommy's got enough weight for two or three daughters."

Eleanor tried to get the front seat to lean forward, but it wouldn't move for her either. It stood rigid as if it was trying to make a statement against all of mankind.

"Maybe I can just push the seat forward, then push it back in place," suggested Eleanor.

"Whatever."

Eleanor got on her knees to feel for the lever underneath the seat to move it forward. After several tries, she found it, then the seat shot forward into the dashboard, causing Eleanor's head to hit the inside panel of the door.

"Are you okay, Mom?"

"I'll be fine. I'm a tough ol' broad. Now help me up."

Vegas helped her mother up, slipped the lamp into the back, moved the seat back into place, helped seat her mother, and took her seat. As she pulled out of the parking spot, the engine stalled.

"Ah! I'm never going to get the hang of this."

"Yes, you will. You're my daughter. You can do anything. Well, maybe not move a seat forward, but other than that, your powers are unlimited. Now let Mommy help. Forward ho, forward ho, forward ho!"

"Mom, that's not helping."

"Words of encouragement from a mother's lips are always helpful." Eleanor smiled at her words. "Oh, that was beautifully said, if I say so myself. That would look good on a big coffee mug. I know I'd buy one, especially since I came up with the slogan. Now, back to work. Forward ho, forward ho, forward ho!"

"This has been a long day," Vegas mumbled as she restarted the vehicle and pulled out. She noticed a large gray

Ford F-550 behind her. It had huge tires, a large winch in front, and wide fenders in the back to cover the tires.

"That is a huge truck behind us," whispered Vegas as she stared in her rearview mirror.

Eleanor tried to turn around, but the seatbelt wouldn't let her.

"I can't see it."

"Why do men make their trucks that big?"

Eleanor unbuckled her seatbelt, and twisted and turned like a magician trying to escape from a box.

"What are you doing?" Vegas asked as she pushed her mother's hips away from her face.

"I'm trying to see the truck."

"It's not that big of a deal, Mom. Now sit back down. Your butt is fogging up my windshield."

Eleanor turned back around in her seat, then attempted to put her seatbelt on, but there wasn't any slack in the belt and she couldn't get it to reach the buckle.

"Something's wrong."

"What?"

"My seatbelt isn't reaching."

"Maybe you put on some weight."

"I had it on a second ago. And I'll have you to know that I'm perfectly balanced for my body frame, although I have to admit that all of my fat goes to my butt."

"Unfortunately you've passed that trait on to the next generation."

"Your father liked my bottom. He called it Magic Mountain."

"I don't want to know that."

Vegas made a right turn.

"Where are you going?" asked Eleanor. "This isn't the way home."

"I'm just testing the ol' Volkswagen here, is all."

"I must test my vehicle all the time, because I'm always getting lost. I really don't like driving in rush hour. It makes me all nervous. You never know who you might meet on the way to anywhere anymore. Could be some crazy person that escaped prison, or a space alien or something like that."

"You think you're going to meet a space alien in Georgia?"

"If they want a nice place to live, of course they'll come to Georgia. We got everything here. Nice weather, good people—"

"Except for the crazy person you were talking about that escaped from prison."

"I'm sure he's from out of state, probably Alabama. You know, I have a theory that no matter where you live in this world, at some point in your life you'll end up in Alabama."

"Have you ever been to Alabama?"

"No. But I've never been in a yellow Volkswagen before either – and with a cat lamp in the backseat. So my Alabama theory is looking more possible every day."

Vegas looked in the mirror and saw the truck turn.

"The truck's gone."

"I guess he's going home," said Eleanor. "Hey, you didn't really think it was following us, did you?"

"I just thought it was interesting that it pulled out when we did and stayed behind us for some time."

"Ah, that's why you took that wrong turn. I wish I knew all of that before. Maybe I could have helped out somehow."

"How would you have done that?"

"I don't know. Hey, maybe I could have thrown the lamp out, it would have shattered, then they'd run over it and get a flat tire and wreck. The police would come and they would be taken by ambulance and end up in the hospital. And we'd have to go there to try and figure out why they were following us, and do you know where the hospital would be?"

"I'm guessing the hospital is in Alabama."

Eleanor began clapping her hands quickly but softly in front of her grinning face. "My theory has already come true. I'm so glad I could share this victorious moment with my baby girl."

Vegas pulled in the Pine Sap Camper Park road entrance and parked the Volkswagen next to her camper. Her and her mother took turns trying to maneuver the lamp out of the backseat. Eleanor finally did it and gave her daughter a gloating smile and placed it in her vehicle. Vegas got the puzzle box out of the trunk, and the two of them went into the camper.

Vegas sat down at the table and opened the puzzle box. Inside there was a manual, and all the pieces looked different in color.

"This looks completely different from the puzzle that Mr. Harper gave me."

"It does look different," said Eleanor. "Maybe they're two different versions of the puzzle. You know, one for young people and one for old people."

"That makes no sense."

"Sometimes the puzzle pieces are larger for children and smaller for adults."

Vegas got the other puzzle box and opened it. She looked inside and compared the two puzzles. "The pieces are the same size."

"Well, I'm sticking to my theory, especially since my Alabama theory already came true tonight."

Vegas stared at both puzzles, comparing them.

"The one we got at the Dixie Discount is much better made, and it has a manual. The one Mr. Harper gave me looks very shoddy."

"Maybe the one he gave you was a, a ... what do you call it."

"Puzzle?"

"No. It's called the first of something. You know like I'm the first of you so that would make me what?"

"Don't bait me, Mom. I'm tired enough to where I just might say it."

"I can't think of the name in which it's the first of something. Oh, shoot, my brain is falling down again."

"Prototype?"

"That's it!" shouted Eleanor.

Vegas looked back at the puzzles. "Something just isn't right here."

CHAPTER 7

VEGAS EMPTIED the pieces of the newer puzzle onto the table. They were black on one side with lines that were drawn at different angles in different locations on each piece. On the other side was a simple light brown cardboard. She picked up the manual and began reading it aloud.

"'Solve the *Riddles & Riches* puzzle and follow the five clues to genuine treasure! Treasure that is valued more than five hundred thousand dollars as of its assembling! Can you find the treasure? Inside this lid is the first clue to your treasure. Upon finding the treasure, call 555-9363. Upon proof that you have found the treasure, you will be given a bonus ten thousand dollars in cash!' I bet they offer the bonus cash so whoever finds it will report it."

"Oh, what I could do with ten thousand dollars," Eleanor said dreamily. "I could finally get that massaging shower I saw advertised on TV one time. It has like ten spray nozzles on it. Taking a shower in that thing would be like being in a car wash. Oh, I'd love that. Beep-beep," she added with a laugh.

"But there are no images on the pieces other than these lines, and neither the box nor the manual shows what the image should be," Vegas said, ignoring her mother.

Eleanor picked up one of the pieces and looked at it closely. "Maybe with all of these lines it's a map."

"Maybe it's a map or maybe it spells out a word or something like that. At least this time I know which side to turn over to look for one. This one has a manual and a phone number to call when you find it. It tells me there are five clues. The other one didn't have any of that."

Vegas felt the puzzle pieces between her index finger and thumb.

"What are you doing?" asked Eleanor. "You act like you're trying to date the puzzle."

"I was wondering if there was an indention, like some sort of braille on it. Let me try something."

Vegas walked to a trunk that was covered with a sheet. She tossed the sheet onto the nearby bed, pulled the trunk into the middle of the floor, opened the lid, and began rummaging through it.

"That's where my trunk went," said Eleanor. "I've been looking all over for that thing. I was going to put my shoes in that and couldn't find the thing. Well, no wonder I couldn't find it, my beautiful daughter stole it."

"I didn't steal it," Vegas said. "You told me to take it because it was in your way. Don't you remember?"

"I don't remember a lot of things. I could hide my own Easter eggs. My strategy would be to put them in one big pile somewhere that I could remember. Oh, I could put them in my pockets."

"How are you going to put a big pile of Easter eggs into your pocket?"

"I'd have to wear my fat pants. If I can hide my big butt in those, then I can hide a big pile of Easter eggs in them. What are you looking for in that trunk anyway?"

"A black light."

"Why?"

Vegas found the light and showed her mother. "Here it is."

"Hooray for baby!" Eleanor clapped. "I'll need to take you on my Easter egg hunt."

"I'm not looking through your pants," Vegas said and took the black light to the table. She turned off the main light and turned on the black light, running it over the puzzle pieces. She apparently wasn't seeing what she was looking for.

"Why did you turn the light off?" asked Eleanor. "I feel like you're trying to get me to leave."

"I've been doing that since I was born."

"Well, you can stop because it's not going to work."

"I thought maybe there was an image on the pieces that could only be seen in a black light, but there isn't anything here."

Vegas turned off the black light and set it down. She flipped on the overhead light and looked at the manual again, hoping to find something, anything that would tip her off.

"There's just nothing here," Vegas said in frustration.

"Maybe it's a big hoax," said Eleanor.

"They could be sued by everyone for fraud if that was the case. Why don't these puzzles match up? The pieces are shaped differently, and they aren't even the same colors. The one that Mr. Harper gave me looks like it must have been a sample model before they went with the one that we got from the Dixie Discount."

Eleanor picked up the puzzle box they got from the Dixie Discount and looked it over. "Well, this one isn't made much better. The label is already starting to peel off."

Vegas suddenly had an epiphany.

"Let me see that," said Vegas.

Vegas took the puzzle top box and looked it over. The label

was beginning to peel at the edge. She carefully began peeling it off.

Underneath was an image of a peach tree.

"That's a nice-looking apple tree," said Eleanor.

"It's not an apple tree. It's a peach tree."

"How do you know it's a peach tree?"

"Because the words 'peach tree' are written on the leaves."

"I never had a peach from a tree. I always got them from a can. I wonder how they taste straight from the tree."

"Maybe I need to think outside the box," mused Vegas.

"You'd be a terrible cat owner," Eleanor said with a laugh. "You know, I'm craving peaches all of the sudden."

Vegas picked up the manual.

"The puzzle pieces aren't the clues. The manual says inside this lid is the first clue to your treasure. The clues are on the box under the label on the lid. The puzzle pieces are just to confuse you. That's why nobody could solve it. They were looking at the wrong thing."

"Oh, this is exciting," Eleanor said, rubbing her hands together. "It's just as exciting when I ate all of those crawdads and won that boot."

Vegas stared at her mother like a dog confused by an empty bowl. "What are you talking about?"

"When I was younger, I entered a crawdad eating contest and won a boot. Those things tasted pretty good until you got to about eighteen. Then they start to lose their flavor."

"The boot?"

"No, the crawdads," Eleanor replied.

"You've led a full life."

"I was full that day anyway."

Vegas looked again at the image of the peach tree. On the upper left corner were the letters EVARB. On the upper right corner were the letters NEM, TSAE was on the bottom left, and KAO was on the bottom right.

"What do these letters stand for?" asked Eleanor.

"I'm not sure," Vegas said as she stared at each group of letters. "Wait. They're spelled backwards. BRAVE MEN EAST OAK."

"Oh, you solved it!" Eleanor said and hugged Vegas. "Mommy is so proud of you. Though I have to admit it sounds like it was written by a six-year old."

"But what does it mean?"

"They're a bunch of brave men in an oak somewhere out east, which is inside a peach tree," said Eleanor. "Can oak trees grow inside peach trees? And how many brave men are there? Surely you could marry one of them."

"Mom, leave my dating life out of this."

"You don't have a dating life. You're dating your work now."

"Atlanta," Vegas said in a whisper.

"What?"

"The peach tree is Atlanta. The brave men are the Atlanta Braves baseball team. There must be an oak tree on the east side of the park somewhere. That's where I'll find the next clue."

Vegas took the puzzle box that Mr. Harper had given her and began looking at the label to see if it would peel off. It wouldn't.

"The puzzle box label Mr. Harper gave me is printed directly on the box. There's no clue under it."

"What does that mean?" asked Eleanor.

"I'm not sure. Maybe Walter Peabody just did an early version of it and there are more of them that the publisher doesn't know about. Or did Mr. Harper give me a bad puzzle box so I couldn't figure it out."

"Why would he do that?"

"I don't know. Maybe he just didn't know there was supposed to be a clue under it to start with."

"Well, we know the answer to the puzzle. We're going to Atlanta."

"What do you mean by we?"

Eleanor stared at her daughter a little heartbroken. "We're a team. Like the Atlanta Braves. Not having me around is like a baseball team without its quarterback."

"Baseball teams don't have quarterbacks."

"Ours does," Eleanor said with a smile.

"Mom, you're going to stay home and I'm going to go and try to figure this out. You can order that showerhead you were talking about or get a book about baseball."

"You're going to go to Atlanta all by yourself?"

"Yes."

"Well, what am I going to do at home?"

"I'll let you take the trunk back, and you can hide your Easter eggs in them."

"I want to come."

"You're going to go home and I'm going to pack my things and head to Atlanta in the morning."

"Well, how long will you be gone?"

"I don't know. It all depends upon the next clue. I might be coming straight back or I might be gone for several days. I'll call you."

"How are you going to do that? You don't own a cellphone."

"I'll call from a motel."

"You're going to stay in a motel?" Eleanor was horrified.

"It's possible."

"I can't let my baby stay in a motel by herself. I need to be with you so you'll have somebody to play with."

"I'm not going there to play, Mom. I'm going to Atlanta on a case. Now go on home. Everything will be okay."

Eleanor reluctantly got up and headed toward the door. She stopped to wrap her arms around her daughter as if she was about to go off to war.

"I'm going to miss you."

"Mom, Atlanta is just a few hours away. Everything will be okay. Now, go home, fix yourself a good dinner, and I'll call you when I get there."

"What are you going to eat?"

"I'll eat something. Don't worry about me."

"But you'll eat a bunch of junk. Come home with me and I'll fix you something good to eat."

"No, Mom, I'll be fine."

"Okay," Eleanor said reluctantly and left.

Vegas went to a cabinet and pulled out a box of Pop Tarts, slid out a package of the tasty treats, opened the wrapper, and ate it while packing her suitcase.

CHAPTER 8

AT SIX THE NEXT MORNING, Vegas clumsily exited her camper carrying a bright-red suitcase with a slightly dented lid. She opened the back of the Volkswagen and started to put her suitcase in when she realized her mistake.

"Why can't I remember the trunk is in the front?" she mumbled as she slammed the engine bay door closed and proceeded to the front of the vehicle, opened the trunk, and threw her suitcase in. She tossed a couple of granola bars onto the front passenger seat as she got in the car, and as she was pulling out, only stalled the engine twice.

Vegas noticed the darkness hanging around a little longer now that it was late August. A sure sign that fall was just around the corner. She attempted to turn on the radio, but the knob came off in her hand. She stared at it for a moment. "I don't believe Pepper told me about this feature," she said aloud and slid the knob back into place.

She reasoned that if she couldn't turn on the radio for music, she would provide her own. She began singing The Beatles' *Blackbird*. Her singing was interrupted by a sound in the back seat.

"Are we there yet?"

"Mom?"

A form rose up and Eleanor wiped the sleep from her eyes. "Yeah, what time is it?"

"It's a little after six in the morning. What are you doing in the car? And did you break my radio knob?"

"I didn't want to be late for our trip."

"*We* weren't going on a trip," Vegas said. "It was just *me*. You were supposed to go home."

Eleanor ignored her. "What were you saying about a radio knob?"

"It came off when I tried to turn on the radio."

"But I heard music playing."

"That was me singing."

"That was you? Oh, baby, you sing divinely. I'll sign you up for music lessons when we get back from our vacation."

"It's not a vacation. I'm on a case."

"Maybe I can fix the radio," Eleanor said as she reached between the front seats and tried to get to the radio. "Woo, Mommy's feeling dizzy."

Vegas gently pushed her back into her seat. "Mom, don't come crawling up here between the seats. You'll make me wreck. Now why are you in my backseat?"

"You just told me to stay back here."

"You know what I mean."

"I can't let my baby go all the way to sin city without me. So I packed my suitcase and rushed right over. You might need my backup."

"I've needed you to back up out of my life for some time now."

"Don't yell at me. You're making me all tense."

"How did you get in the car? Did I not lock it?"

It was quiet for a few seconds - Vegas knew something was

wrong. Eleanor whispered, "The passenger side door doesn't work now."

"Why? What do you mean?"

"I used a coat hanger to unlock it, and I think I messed it up. Here, let me come up there so we can talk." Eleanor climbed into the front seat, getting stuck twice before managing to get in the passenger seat upside down.

"Mom, what are you doing?"

"Vegas, I'm getting carsick," Eleanor said before sliding down to the floorboard.

"You have to turn right side up. You're going to make me crash the car."

Eleanor got her legs turned around and into Vegas' line of sight. "Mom, your feet are up my nose!"

"I'm sorry. I feel like I've fallen in the commode or something. All I need now is the splash."

"Mom, you have to get up from there."

"I'm not down here for sport, Vegas."

"Do I need to pull over?"

After much effort, Eleanor finally got situated properly in the passenger seat. "Oh, man, I forgot my water."

Eleanor started to climb back into the back when Vegas stopped her. "You're not going back there as long as the vehicle is moving."

"But I'm thirsty."

"You're also crazy."

"Well, the first one is causing the second one."

"How long have you been back there anyhow?"

"I got in around midnight, I guess. I can't remember for sure because my cellphone is in my purse in the back."

"What if I thought you were a carjacker or something and came out and hurt you? I'd never forgive myself."

"Carjacker," Eleanor said with a laugh. "Honey, nobody is

going to steal this car. The radio doesn't work and the passenger door is messed up."

"I'm going to take you home."

"No," said Eleanor as she crossed her arms in defiance. "I refuse to go back home. I'll just follow you in my vehicle. I'm a rebel mom."

"What is wrong with you?"

"Honey, that list is loooong," Eleanor said with a loud laugh.

Vegas said angrily, "I can't believe this is happening. Why can't I have a normal mom?"

"They don't make those, sweetie," said Eleanor. "How long will it take us to get to Atlanta anyway?"

"It depends on the traffic."

"Too bad we can't travel by some sort of portal. I saw on TV last night that you can travel through time portals. It's science, honey."

"There are no portals."

"Is it because of the microchip shortage?"

Vegas did a double take. "What?"

"I saw on the news that there's some sort of huge microchip shortage and nobody can get any for their cars or cornflakes or anything."

"There are no such thing as portals."

"That's where you're wrong. I saw that TV show that Pepper was talking about. What was it called? ... *Ancient Aliens*! They said that aliens travel through portals all the time."

"No, they don't."

"Then how do they get here?"

"They don't. What on earth happened to the History Channel anyway?"

"I just think–"

"Mom, I need you to stop talking. I'm already exhausted."

Eleanor lifted her hands up as if she was backing away from the dinner table before the snails arrived. "I understand. You're concentrating on your case. You're not trying to be mean to Mommy. I don't take any offense, and I forgive you for your tone of voice."

"Mom, I'm not being mean. You broke into my vehicle and slept here, then proceeded to scare me to death. I had some granola bars on the front seat, by the way. What did you do with them?"

Eleanor began looking around. "I thought I heard something fall when I came from the back. I think they're under the seat here."

Eleanor felt under the seat and pulled out both bars.

"Mommy found them! How do you eat these things, anyway? They are as dry as a desert."

Vegas took one and opened it. "They help me get through the day."

"Why don't we stop at Hardees' and get you a sausage and biscuit? That's what real Southern girls eat in the morning."

"I don't have time for that."

"You have to make time to eat. See, this is why I slept in your vehicle last night - you don't take care of yourself when you're obsessed with a case."

"It's not an obsession. It's simply my job, and I want to get started and concentrate on it so I can figure it out for my client."

"Speaking of which, did you figure out why the puzzles don't match?"

"No. The only thing that makes sense is that it could have been a prototype and Mr. Harper wasn't aware of it."

"Did it say prototype on the box?"

"No, but that doesn't mean it wasn't."

"Did you call Mr. Harper about it?"

"Not yet. I want to see what we find at the tree today first. Then I'll call."

Eleanor asked, "When you call him, can you tell him about my book?"

"What book?"

"I'm thinking about writing a book."

"About what?"

"I'm not sure. That's my only problem."

"That's not your only problem, Mom."

"Well, maybe a kid's book of some kind, something with dinosaurs in it. Kids like dinosaurs, don't they?"

"Some do, I'm sure. But do you know anything about dinosaurs?"

"No, but that's what the book's for."

"Have you ever read anything about dinosaurs?"

"Not yet. But it's called research, Vegas. That's how authors learn. Oh, I got it! I'll call it *Wally the Dinosaur*. He could be a dog."

Vegas shook her head. "Mom, dogs aren't dinosaurs."

"This one is. He could be gigantic, too. Maybe I can even illustrate the book. I'll make Wally green, and he'll play fetch, and his owner will be a little cave girl named ... uh, what is a good cave girl's name?"

Vegas sighed. "This is going to be the longest trip of my life."

"Great, it'll give us time to talk," Eleanor said with a smile.

CHAPTER 9

VEGAS PULLED her Volkswagen into the empty parking lot of the Atlanta Braves baseball stadium at just after noon.

"This place is huge," Eleanor observed as she stared out the windshield.

"The stadium seats a lot of people, so they have to have a large parking lot."

"I'd hate to have to wash all their dishes after they eat their hot dogs. I hate washing mine, for crying out loud, and it's just one of me. But you're welcome over any time. I'd happily wash your dishes."

"Thanks, Mom," Vegas said as she stared at the vast paved area.

"I guess we have to hurry before the game starts."

"They're playing away this week, so that's not going to be a problem. Now, which way is east?"

The two of them sat in the Volkswagen in the middle of the parking lot looking about aimlessly.

"Your father always told me that the sun rises in the east and sets in the west. We had a flower pot on the back deck, and that way was east. The outbuilding was west. That's the easiest way to remember it."

Vegas turned slowly to her mother. "There's no flower pot or outbuilding here, Mom."

Eleanor pondered her daughter's words. "That could be a problem."

"The riddle was BRAVE MEN EAST OAK. So there's a group of trees over there. Let's try them."

Vegas drove to the outcrop of trees. Vegas got out, but Eleanor couldn't get her door to open.

"Vegas, it won't open."

Vegas walked over to the passenger side door and tried pulling it open. "Is it locked?"

"I think I messed something up when I broke into it last night with the coat hanger."

"I can't believe you," Vegas said with frustration. "I just got the vehicle and you messed up the door."

"I wouldn't have messed it up if you had just let me come with you in the first place."

Vegas tried again to open the door, but it wouldn't budge. In surrender she shouted, "Well, you're going to have to come out the driver's side."

"I can't do that. I'm not built for maneuvering around obstacles. Besides, it wouldn't be lady-like."

"You've got no choice, and you're no lady. Besides, you didn't have any trouble sliding into the front seat this morning when I was driving down the road. I'm going to get the folding shovel out of the trunk." Vegas walked to the rear of the vehicle and mumbled, "Man, what is it with women?"

Vegas saw Eleanor crawling over the gearshift as she opened the rear hatch. She made a sound like a pirate rolling her Rs before she slammed the engine bay lid closed and walked to the trunk in the front.

As Vegas opened the trunk, the Volkswagen began drifting forward.

"Mom, the vehicle's moving!"

Vegas got out of the way as the Volkswagen drifted into a tree and Eleanor slid out the driver's side door and onto the pavement. Vegas quickly went to her mother.

"Mom, are you okay?"

Eleanor blinked her eyes quickly several times. "What happened?"

"You must have knocked the vehicle out of gear, and that made it move forward," Vegas said and helped her mother off the ground.

"That, I have to say, was a bit exhilarating," Eleanor said with a nervous laugh. "You can't have that kind of excitement back at the house washing dishes."

Vegas shook her head in despair. "You could have been hurt. See, this is why I wish you would stop breaking into my vehicle and hiding so that you can always be with me. You're like a puppy that follows behind me when I go to the store. I'm going to have to start pinning you up or something."

Vegas walked to the front of the vehicle and looked it over.

"Is it damaged?" asked a penitent Eleanor.

"It doesn't seem to be. Maybe a few scratches are all."

Vegas got into the vehicle, started it up, and backed it away from the trees before proceeding to get into the trunk and pulling out her bag. She unzipped it and began rummaging through her stuff.

"Are you going to camp out here or something?"

"No, I'm looking for my folding shovel."

"Folding shovel? Most women pack a makeup kit when they go on a trip, but not my daughter. She packs a folding shovel when she goes traveling. Even I think that's weird, and I'm your mother."

"I also seem to always pack a crazy woman with me when I go on a road trip," Vegas added with emphasis.

Vegas found the shovel and pulled it out and showed her mother. "I knew I brought it." Vegas walked to the trees, unfolded the shovel, and began poking the blade into the ground.

"Where did you get a folding shovel?"

"Every girl needs a gun and a shovel in case things get out of hand."

"That's an interesting motto. I'm learning quite a bit about you on our little vacation here."

"It's not a vacation. I'm on a case. I'm the only private investigator in the world that ends up with their mother on a case. You've got to stop doing that. All the other investigators are going to laugh at me."

"Their mothers won't laugh at you. They'll give you an ole atta girl pat on the back. What are you poking the ground for anyway?"

"I'm looking for the next clue to our puzzle."

"What exactly are we looking for?"

"We'll know it when we find it. Ah, man, I just broke my shovel," said Vegas.

"It happens. Now, how will we know we found the clue?" asked Eleanor. "I mean, we could find an empty Coke can and think that's a clue, but it actually isn't, so we'd end up going in the wrong direction. This could happen, you know. Well, unless it is a clue, then we'd be going in the right direction. Do you think the clue will be a Coke can?"

"I really don't, Mom." Vegas prodded the ground with the shovel handle and hit something metallic. The mother and daughter team looked at each other in wonder.

"Is that it?" asked Eleanor.

"I guess we're about to find out."

Vegas began digging with her hands.

"What is it?"

"I don't know yet."

"You don't think it's a bomb, do you?"

Vegas stopped digging and stared at her mother. "Why are you putting that thought into my head?"

"Well, maybe he just didn't want anyone to solve the puzzle, so he planted bombs at each clue site."

"That would be a strange business plan, don't you think?"

"It would add some excitement to the hunt."

Vegas dug some more and found a plastic bag. She lifted it up and saw a metal container the size of a cake pan with a hinged lid on top. She took it out of the bag and tried to open it.

"Is that the clue?"

"I'm guessing it is," said Vegas as she turned the box over and saw the words RIDDLES & RICHES CLUE #2 written on it. "Oh, this is it!"

"This is so exciting!" Eleanor shouted. "What do you think it is? Maybe there's gold inside."

"Mom, this is the second clue. We have to find five. They wouldn't put the treasure in the second clue."

"I guess that's true. I wish there was a man inside there for you. That would be my treasure."

"He'd be a bit small, don't you think?"

"I'm sure we could stretch him out a bit. How do you open it?"

"I'm not sure. Wait, the top slides off. It's rusted on."

Vegas took her shovel and began beating on the end of the top until it slid forward enough, then used her hands to pull it open. Inside was a plaque that read HORSES AND PROBLEMS 3.

"Horses and Problems 3?" Vegas asked. She looked at the plaque like it was a computer date who had obviously used somebody else's photo in their posting.

Eleanor took the plaque and looked at it. "Horses and Problems 3. I wonder what that means?"

"We need to get photos of this and write down the coordinates, then put it back. I'll get my camera."

"Oh, no need," said Eleanor. "I can use my phone." She began digging around in her large purse for her phone before she finally found it next to her oven mitt. She began taking photos of Vegas.

"You're not supposed to take photos of me. You're supposed to take them of the clues."

"Well, this is the first time I've ever taken a photo of something I dug up before. It's kind of exciting."

After taking the photos of the clue and the surrounding area, Vegas buried everything again, and smoothed down the dirt. Then they managed to get the coordinates from Eleanor's phone.

"Now we have to figure out what Horses and Problems 3 means, and–" But before Vegas could finish her thought, she saw a large Ford 550 in the far end of the parking lot.

"What is it?" asked Eleanor.

"That truck. That's the one that pulled out behind us when we left the Dixie Discount."

Eleanor stared at the truck, using her hand to shield her eyes. "That can't be the same truck."

"Yes, it is. It's silver, it has large tires, and it has a big bumper with a winch. That's the same truck I saw following us last night."

"Why would they follow us?"

"They want the clues."

"Should we leave?"

"I'm guessing we better."

They hurried to the Volkswagen. Vegas put her shovel into

the trunk while her mother struggled with the passenger door, but it still wouldn't open.

Vegas said, "You have to get in through the driver's side."

Eleanor wobbled around to the driver's side and crawled over the driver's seat and across the gearshift.

"Honey, I'm stuck."

"This is the slowest getaway ever!" Vegas shouted in frustration.

Vegas carefully reached around her mother's posterior and released her pant pocket from where it was snagged on the gearshift.

"How did this happen anyway?"

"I get hung up on everything. I'm like a big glue gun."

Vegas turned her head and saw the large truck driving slowly toward them. She started the vehicle, slammed the door closed and pulled out, stalling the engine instantly.

"What happened?" asked Eleanor. "Are we out of gas?"

"I killed the engine. Who invented straight shifts anyway?"

"They're coming toward us, Vegas! Should I flash them?" Eleanor asked as she started to raise her shirt.

"Keep your shirt down! We don't want to kill anybody!"

Vegas got the vehicle restarted and took off out of the parking lot and onto the road. Her mother tried rolling the window down to watch the truck, but it only went halfway. Vegas adjusted her rearview mirror to keep an eye on the truck, too, and it promptly fell off onto the floor.

"Oh, my Lord, they're shooting at us!" Eleanor screamed as she pulled her head back inside.

"That was just my mirror," Vegas said.

"They shot your mirror off?"

"Nobody's shooting! It just fell off."

"Your vehicle must be so excited that its mirror popped off."

"I'm guessing what happened is that *somebody* kicked it trying to get into the vehicle."

Eleanor turned around and put her knees in her seat to look through the back window. "I'll be your rearview mirror, honey. They're getting closer. How fast are you going?"

"Fifty-five."

"Step on it!"

Vegas floored the gas pedal.

"How fast are you going now?" asked Eleanor.

"Forty-three."

"We're doing something wrong. Oh, I see the mirror under your feet. I'll get it."

"No, Mom, you'll make me wreck."

Eleanor maneuvered around, her feet against the ceiling and the side of her face against the gearshift, as her right arm searched for the mirror.

"Mom, get up from there. That's my foot you're grabbing!"

"You need your mirror, baby. You have to know what is going on behind you."

Vegas shook her head. "I'm trapped in a weird life."

"Mommy will get you through it."

"You're the one that keeps throwing me into it."

"I got the mirror," Eleanor said, and as she sat up, she hit the gearshift, sending the engine from fourth gear to second, which caused the vehicle to do some sort of backward rev that it wasn't meant to do, and caused the back tires to do a quick burnout.

"What are you doing?" screamed Vegas.

"I'm getting your mirror. Mission accomplished, by the way," Eleanor said, holding it up for Vegas to see. "It might need washing, though."

"You've put me in the wrong gear."

Vegas got the car up to speed again, and Eleanor looked through the back window.

"Hey, the truck's gone."

"We probably scared them to death. Are you sure they're gone?"

"Yeah, see," Eleanor said and handed her daughter the rearview mirror.

"I can use my driver's side mirror, thanks," replied Vegas. "Where did it go?"

"I don't know, but I have to say that was very exciting. It never occurred to me that when I come with you from now on that I should wear pants without pockets. Thank God for sweatpants."

"First, you didn't come with me. You're a stowaway. You weren't supposed to be here to start with."

"Without me you wouldn't have your mirror off the floor."

"Without you it would still be where it's supposed to be."

"Do we go back home now?"

"No. Our clue of Horses and Problems 3 might be for something here in Atlanta."

"So what do we do?"

"We get a room for the night and try to figure things out."

"Oh, boy, it'll be like nerd camping."

CHAPTER 10

VEGAS AND ELEANOR pulled into a motel called The Lazy Susan. It had a large sign shaped like a palm tree on the top of the building. Inside the lines of the palm tree were the words The Lazy Susan lit up with a hula girl that appeared to be doing the hula. Vegas pulled into a parking spot in front of the main office and shut off the engine. Vegas got out of the car and stretched her arms high above her head. She then held the driver's side door open so her mother could crawl out.

"Can you get out, Mom?"

"I don't see why not. I did it before."

"You also knocked it out of gear and it rolled forward into a tree. You can't roll forward here or you'll end up in the main office, and I'm pretty sure they're not going to give us a room after that."

Eleanor grunted and groaned as she made her way out of the vehicle, this time without causing any damage. Vegas then shut the door and they looked at The Lazy Susan.

"It's not much of a motel, is it?" asked Vegas. "Nice hula dancer, though. It looks like they spent all their money on their sign instead of the motel."

"It'll do. I'm pretty tired. I've never searched for treasure and got chased by bandits in a baseball parking lot before. It takes a lot out of a girl."

"It's been an interesting day, that's for sure. It doesn't look like there's anybody else staying here."

"It's our second straight empty parking lot," observed Eleanor. "Everybody must find out we're coming and make a run for the hills. Or do you think it's abandoned?"

Eleanor and Vegas stared at the main office and the dilapidated condition it was in. "It looks like it should be," said Vegas. "Let's go to the office and find out."

Eleanor suddenly stopped.

"What's wrong?" asked Vegas.

"I thought I heard something."

"What?"

"I'm not sure. It was almost like a child crying."

The two of them stood still, looking like some sort of mime convention where they both forgot to bring their invisible door. Vegas said, "I don't hear anything."

Eleanor cupped her right ear with her right hand. "I was positive I heard a child cry."

"There's nothing here but a Pepsi machine and traffic going by. Maybe a kid cried from down the road because their mother wouldn't leave them alone either. Now, come on."

Vegas opened the door to the motel office, which caused the bell overhead to jingle. Upon entering, they saw a tall woman, well over six feet, probably in her early forties, standing behind the counter.

"Hello," the woman said in a husky, displeased voice.

"Hello," Vegas said.

"Do you need a room?" the woman asked after a pause.

"Do you have one with two beds?" asked Vegas.

"We only have one room available, on the end. The others

have been closed by the building inspector because of some sort of red ooze coming down the wall."

"Red ooze?" Eleanor and Vegas asked simultaneously. They stared at each other wondering if they should run away.

"It's not toxic or anything like that. It's just odd."

"Do they have any idea what it is?" asked Vegas.

"No. But that's what the tests are for. Room seven on the end is ooze-free, though, so I can offer you that one. However, if you have some adventure in you, I can give you one with the ooze. I'll have to charge you more, though, to help pay for both the thrill fee and the higher insurance premium."

Vegas stared at the woman as she tried to figure out if she was kidding. "I think we'll take the ooze-free room on the end."

The woman reached under the counter and pulled out the registry book. She opened it up and handed Vegas a pen. "Sign in here."

Vegas took the pen and signed in. She couldn't help but notice the last person to sign in was over a month ago.

"Can I sign it, too?" asked Eleanor.

"You're not even supposed to be here."

"Let her sign it, too," said the woman behind the counter.

"Encouraging her isn't going to make our lives any easier," Vegas said before she surrendered and gave her mother the pen.

Eleanor signed her name. "I wish I had a prettier signature. Mine looks too normal. Wait, I misspelled Eleanor. Can I have another piece of paper?"

"It's a registry, Mom, not a test."

"But I misspelled my name. I left the 'a' out. What if a crime takes place and I go missing? They'll look at the registry and say that it wasn't me because I misspelled my name."

"I think your misspelling your name would be proof that it was you," said Vegas.

"I do this on my checks, too," said Eleanor. "I always mess something up."

"Don't worry about it, Mom," Vegas said as she took the pen from her mother and set it on the counter beside the registry.

The woman turned to the wall behind her where room keys were hung.

"Are you the Susan on the sign?" asked Eleanor.

"No," she said as she turned around with a room key in her hand. "I'm the Lazy on the sign. My mother is the Susan. She's retired now. Please don't tell her about the ooze. She used to jump motorcycles when she was in college."

"That's impressive," said Eleanor. "I used to have a blue bicycle with a basket on the front, and I tried to jump a row of baby dolls, but I chickened out. I wasn't in college, though."

"Did she jump cars or buses or something?" asked Vegas.

"No, you misunderstood. She literally jumped over motorcycles. She used a unicycle."

"You can jump motorcycles with a unicycle?" asked Vegas.

"Not every time. She had trouble building up enough speed to get up the ramp. Those things really need another wheel on 'em."

"Then they'd be called bicycles," said Vegas.

"I don't care what you call them, they need another wheel," Lazy said as she looked at the key in her hand. "That's not the right key." She turned back around and retrieved the key, then handed it to Vegas.

"Here's your key. It says five on it, but it's really for room seven."

"Interesting system," said Vegas.

Eleanor said, "I once had a plaid-colored case that said

sewing kit on it, but I kept my Pepto Bismol and vacuum cleaner bags in it."

"That's an odd combination, Mom."

"You use what you can find," said Eleanor.

"She's a girl on the go," said Lazy. "Are you two just staying the night?"

"Yeah, we'll hit the road tomorrow morning."

"How early are you going to leave?"

"Around six o'clock."

"Six comes in the morning, too?" Lazy asked.

"Yeah, if you time it right," said Vegas. "How much do you charge for one night?"

"Seventy-five dollars."

Eleanor handed Lazy a credit card.

"What are you doing?" asked Vegas.

"I'm paying for the room."

"I can pay for the room," Vegas said as she began feeling around her pockets for cash.

Lazy looked at Vegas and said, "I'll just take this credit card, because you look like all you're doing is scratching."

Lazy took the card and swiped it, then handed it back to Eleanor.

"There is nothing wrong with a mother paying for her and her daughter's room on vacation," said Eleanor.

"Especially when the daughter apparently doesn't have any money," stated Lazy.

Vegas ignored them and asked, "Is there a place to eat around here?"

Eleanor interrupted, "Oh, I got food for us. I brought it with me last night."

"What did you bring?" asked Lazy.

"*Why* did she bring it is the better question," said Vegas.

"I knew you wouldn't take time to go out and eat, so I

brought some goodies with me. I got a whole pack of Fifth Avenue candy bars. Well, minus three, because I couldn't get to sleep in your Volkswagen last night and Mommy had herself a little snack."

"You made your mother sleep in your Volkswagen last night?" asked Lazy.

"No. She broke into my Volkswagen so I would bring her with me."

"Why wouldn't you want to bring your mother with you on vacation?" asked Lazy.

"It's not a vacation," said Vegas. "She also messed up my door when she broke into my vehicle."

"I wouldn't have messed up your door if you had left it unlocked."

"Why would I leave it unlocked?"

"So I could get in it."

"I don't understand why you wouldn't want to bring your mother with you on vacation," Lazy said.

Eleanor began to say, "See, we're looking for a–"

Vegas immediately interrupted her mother. "We need to hurry and get to the room now, Mom."

"Why?"

"I'm craving me some Fifth Avenue candy bars. It's the supper of champions."

"Okay," said Eleanor. "Well, it was nice talking to you, Lazy. Is that your real name?"

"It's a nickname."

"I wish I had a nickname," Eleanor said.

"I'll start calling you Thumper," Vegas said as she escorted her mother out the door.

CHAPTER 11

VEGAS AND ELEANOR made their way to room seven. They passed the Pepsi machine and a hole in the sidewalk with the remains of what appeared to be a red sucker inside it. When they got to the door, Vegas noticed that several feet away, there was a steep drop-off into the woods.

"I hope the bank here doesn't give way tonight and we end up down in that ravine," observed Vegas.

Eleanor looked down into the ravine and nervously said, "I'm sure it's safe."

"They have ooze coming down their walls. I'm guessing safety is somewhere around priority twenty-four," said Vegas as she slid the key into the lock of the room seven door. She twisted the key one way, then the other, but it wouldn't unlock. "Come on," she grunted in frustration like a fat man trying to eat the last pieces of cereal with a fork.

"Let me try," said Eleanor.

Vegas stepped out of the way and raised her hands up in frustration. Eleanor twisted the key and rammed her shoulder into the door several times, looking like a hockey player making a point to the other team. Suddenly the door gave way, and Eleanor lost her balance and tumbled inside.

"Are you okay?" Vegas asked as she hurried inside to help her mother up.

"I'm fine. I knew I could get us in. I just had to show it some Eleanor attitude."

"What's with you and doors?" Vegas asked. She found a light switch and flipped it on.

The room held a single bed and had Spider-Man wallpaper and dark-red carpet.

"Looks like either a ten-year-old boy or a forty-year-old man decorated this room," observed Vegas.

"Remember when you used to have Strawberry Cupcake wallpaper?"

"I was five, and I wasn't in the motel business at the time."

"I remember when you ran through the house shouting you were a red tornado and tripped and hit the wall and broke your toe? Those were good times," Eleanor said and placed her head lovingly on her daughter's shoulder.

"What does that have to do with anything?"

"Vacations are for memories."

"We're not on a vacation, Mom. I'm on a case. Remember?"

"I think you need a vacation. You seemed stressed. Like back in the office there, what was your hurry anyway?" asked Eleanor. "Lazy wanted to talk. She might have needed to let out her deepest secrets to unburden her soul or something. She's going to think I'm a crazy woman."

"Mom, everybody that meets you thinks you're a crazy woman. I got you out of there because I didn't want you telling her that we were looking for ... you know," Vegas said and tilted her head up and rolled her eyes to the left.

Eleanor looked at her daughter, unsure what she was implying. Vegas whispered, "Treasure."

"Oh, you think she might conk us over the head and steal it."

"We don't have it to steal yet, but I'm sure she might have got interested in us real fast. You can't trust anybody when it comes to treasure."

"You can trust me," said Eleanor.

"I trust you, I just don't understand you. Now, you stay here and I'll bring the Volkswagen over and park it in front of the door, and you promise me not to break anymore doors."

"I can do that. I'm going to go to the bathroom."

"Roger that."

"Honey," Eleanor said in a concerned voice.

"What?"

"I have to tell you something and I don't know how you'll take it."

Concern crossed Vegas' face. "What is it?"

"Promise me you won't get mad."

"Is something wrong?"

"I don't really like the nickname Thumper."

Vegas sighed with relief. "That's what you're concerned about?"

"I didn't want it to hurt your feelings, but I can't really have a mother-daughter moment now because I have to go to the bathroom," Eleanor said as she hurried to the bathroom and closed the door.

"Okay, bathroom girl."

"I don't like that nickname either!" Eleanor shouted from behind the closed door.

"You don't get to pick your nicknames!" Vegas shouted back and walked out of the room.

As Vegas headed toward the Volkswagen, she saw the large Ford pickup truck. She quickly ducked behind the Pepsi machine. After a few seconds, the truck backed out of the parking lot and headed west onto the highway. Vegas was about to leave her hiding place when she heard a noise coming from the soda machine that she couldn't explain. It sounded like wheezing.

"You sound like you need an inhaler," she whispered to the machine. She then walked to her car and was about to get in when she looked at the office. Maybe the truck driver had gone in. This could be her chance to learn something about him. She walked to the office and went inside. "Lazy? Are you in here?"

There was no response, so Vegas walked around the desk and grabbed the registry. Her mother was the last to register. She shook her head in frustration and went back out and drove her Volkswagen in front of room seven.

She paused before going in. Where did Lazy go? she wondered. Vegas got their luggage then went inside the room and closed the door.

She saw her mother sitting on the bed with candy bars, granola bars, and a bottle of water for each of them.

"Supper is ready, my lady," Eleanor announced in a poor imitation of an English accent.

Vegas set the luggage down by the bed and said, "I need to borrow your phone."

"Why?"

"I'm going to call Mr. Harper and tell him how the case is going," Vegas said as she opened her suitcase and found his business card.

Eleanor went to her purse and began digging for her phone. She pulled out a hairbrush, a small stuffed plush elephant, and a box of chocolate covered cherries before she found her cellphone. "You know, I think it's time you get your own phone."

Vegas took the phone and thought it over. "I think you're right."

"Really?" asked her surprised mother.

"I can't ask you to stop coming on my cases then keep

using your credit cards and cellphone when you do. My hatred of technology is going to have to be put on hold."

"Then you can get rid of the awful payphone in front of your camper and maybe move into a real house."

"Let's not get crazy. Let me advance into the twentieth century first and get comfortable there before I go into the twenty-first century."

Vegas called the number on the card. After four rings, it was answered with a muffled "Hello?"

"Mr. Harper?"

"Yes."

"This is Vegas Chantly. I'm working on the Riddle and Riches case for you and your company."

"Yes. Have you found anything yet?"

"I solved the first clue."

"What? How did you do that?" he said in disbelief.

"First thing is: Where did you get the puzzle that you gave me?"

"It was in storage with all the other books we have. It was the last one."

"Was it a prototype?"

"I have no idea. This was kind of Walter's baby, so he oversaw everything. I told him he had to keep one puzzle for the company to keep on file, so that's why it was in our storage facility."

Vegas informed him, "I bought another puzzle and was able to figure out that the first clue wasn't the puzzle itself, but was hidden under the label on the box. That led me to the next clue at the Atlanta Braves field. I can't remember the name of the field."

"Field of Dreams," volunteered Eleanor.

Vegas shook her head at her mother as Eleanor added, "Yes, it was. I'm very observant, and my mind is like a steel trap. That's why I'm so good at crossword puzzles. But for some reason, I do the down clues better than the across clues. I wonder why that is."

"Because you read up and down," whispered Vegas before turning her attention back to Mr. Harper. "The puzzle I bought was better made than the one you gave me, and there was a clue hidden under the box top. That wasn't on the one you gave me, so that's what made me wonder if it was a prototype."

Mr. Harper stuttered, "I - I - I'm afraid I don't know anything about that. I truly apologize. How did you know to get another one?"

"I just saw it at a store, and the box looked different than the one you gave me, so I decided to get it and check it out."

"I found the clue beneath the label," whispered Eleanor. "I noticed you didn't mention that to him."

Vegas shook her head at her mother.

"What is the next clue?" asked Mr. Harper.

"Horses and Problems 3. Do you have any idea what that means?"

"No. It doesn't ring a bell."

"Well, I'll keep trying to figure it out. I'll call you later."

"Yes, please do. You've advanced this puzzle further than anybody else that I know. I'm very impressed with your skills."

"Thank you. Talk to you again soon."

"Thank you. I'll be looking forward to it."

Vegas ended the call and handed the phone to her mother.

"Now what do we do?" asked Eleanor.

"Try and figure out what Horses and Problems 3 means."

"That doesn't even make sense. I wonder how you would write that out in a crossword puzzle."

"What do you mean?"

"Can you use actual numbers in a crossword puzzle?"

"No. It would mess up the rest of the words. Any numbers would have to be spelled out."

"Maybe I can do a crossword puzzle and make it all numbers."

"That's not a crossword puzzle. That's math."

"I'm terrible at math."

Eleanor reached over on the bed and got the candy bars and bottles of water and handed one of each to her daughter.

"Not much of a dinner, is it?" asked Eleanor.

"We can go out and get something to eat."

"I thought you wanted to stay in."

"I've got to get out and do some thinking. I think well when I'm eating supper."

"This is supper."

"This is a snack. This is what I eat in the middle of the night when I didn't eat my supper."

"Why didn't you eat your supper?"

"Sometimes work gets in the way."

"You work too much. You need to get out and enjoy life some, too. You can't work all the time."

"It's what I like doing."

"But you need to meet someone. You know, get a husband and settle down."

"Apparently I already have someone to settle down with."

"Who?"

"You. Now let's go get some supper."

CHAPTER 12

VEGAS AND ELEANOR pulled into the Big Chicken parking lot a little after seven in the evening. Vegas got out and Eleanor again climbed out of the driver's side door behind her.

"You are going to have to get the passenger door fixed," suggested Eleanor.

"You were the one that broke it, so that's on you."

They both took in the large chicken statue out front. It was at least ten feet tall and made of cast iron. It hovered over them like something from an H.G. Wells novel.

"That's a big chicken," observed Vegas.

"Could you imagine trying to cook a real one like that? You'd have to do it outside, because there's no way it's going to fit into the kitchen."

"I'm guessing you'll need a big frying pan."

"You could cook it in a big pot," said Eleanor.

"I want my chicken fried."

"Fried food isn't that good for you, Vegas."

"It probably doesn't really matter, because I seriously doubt that I'm going to survive trying to catch a giant chicken."

They both looked at the monstrous chicken again, and Eleanor blurted out, "You have to take my picture next to it."

"Can't we just get something to eat?"

"That's not how you do vacations, Vegas."

"You're the one on vacation, and it's interrupting my case. Why can't you understand that?"

"Oh, it's not going to take long. You can take my photo and then we'll solve this little case of yours."

Eleanor searched for her cellphone in her purse and eventually found it between her coupon book – which she had been looking for over a month – and her hand sanitizer. Eleanor looked at the phone. "Oh, Pepper sent his phone number to us in case we need him."

"He has your contact information?"

"We like to keep tabs on you," said Eleanor as she handed her cellphone to her daughter. Vegas accepted it begrudgingly.

"How should I pose?" asked Eleanor.

"The chicken doesn't care."

"But the Eleanor does. I could open my mouth like I'm trying to eat it," Eleanor said with a laugh and opened her mouth wide.

"You just look like you're yelling at it."

"Get in my frying pan, chicken!" Eleanor yelled and started laughing uncontrollably.

An elderly couple came down the street and stopped to watch Eleanor. Vegas hollered to them, "I don't know her!"

Eleanor finally got her laughing under control and posed with her hands on her hips. Vegas took the photo and gave the phone back to her mother.

"This is the best vacation ever," Eleanor said. Vegas shook her head and said nothing.

They walked toward the small window of the restaurant, which was a converted hauling trailer with a couple of picnic tables to each side of it. Nobody else was in the parking lot. When they got to the window, they saw a teenage boy wearing a chicken outfit.

"Welcome to Big Chicken. I'm August, how can I help you?"

"Well, August, this might come as a big surprise to you, but I've never been to Big Chicken before. What do you recommend?"

"McDonalds."

Without missing a beat, Vegas said, "I guess if they make you dress like a chicken, they deserve the anger." She looked at the menu on the wall behind August's head and said, "How about the chicken leg platter to go."

"Coming right up – oh, do you want anything to drink?"

"I'll take a Diet Coke. What about you, Mom?"

"I want a strawberry milkshake."

"That's a little heavy with chicken legs isn't it?"

"I'm a heavy girl."

"Diet Coke and a strawberry milkshake for the heavy girl," August said.

August got to frying and pouring as Vegas and Eleanor walked to the picnic table beneath a floodlight that was nailed to a four-by-four wooden post that leaned to the right. They sat down to wait for their order.

The traffic drove by at a casual pace. The air was warm, and in the distance, they could hear frogs croaking.

"This is kind of nice," observed Eleanor.

"It is nice and quiet here. The giant chicken gives it a country setting."

"Have you thought more about the case?" asked Eleanor.

"Yeah, let me see your phone."

Eleanor began digging around for her phone again.

"Have you lost it already?"

"You don't have to worry, I always find it. Oh, do you need any ChapStick?"

"No, Mom, my lips are fine."

"Looks like I have four in here. I'll give you one," Eleanor said and handed a ChapStick to her daughter, then went back to digging in her purse. She pulled out the hand sanitizer and pointed it at her daughter. "Give Mommy your hands."

"Mom, I'm not a child."

"You also don't have clean hands. Now let me spray you like a skunk," Eleanor said and laughed loudly. Vegas stretched her hands out and Eleanor sprayed them, then put the bottle back into her bottomless purse. She soon found her cellphone and handed it to Vegas. "It might need charging. It's had a long day."

"We all need charging."

Vegas began browsing the internet and Eleanor asked, "What are you looking for?"

"Walter Peabody. Here it is. It says he was born in 1957. He is best known for the *Riddle and Riches* puzzle game in which a person must solve the puzzle and follow the clues which lead to a treasure. It says here that some people believe it's a fraud. It also says he disappeared in 2021."

"Do you think the treasure is the reason he disappeared?"

"I can't help but think that. He knew where the treasure was, so it could have happened. It's not one hundred percent, of course. People disappear for other reasons, too, but you have to think the treasure played a role. Says here he was born and raised in Georgia in a small town called Flat Bottom."

"That's an interesting name for a town. I once heard of a town called Fart, but they officially pronounced it as Farte'. But everybody just called it Fart. They had a race track there, and your father liked to go when you were little."

"I don't remember going to Farte' to watch racing."

"He went by himself. I have that effect on people – they want to leave me behind." Eleanor started laughing. "Did I just make a funny? Leave me *behind* to go to a town called *Fart*. Get it? I just love this vacation."

Vegas ignored her mother and continued reading. After a moment, she said, "Listen to this. It says he was raised on a small horse ranch named – you won't believe this – Horses and Problems."

"Hey, I've heard of that! But didn't the clue have a three in it?"

"Your order is ready!" August shouted from his tiny window.

"We'll be right there!" Vegas shouted back.

"Good, because I'm not coming out dressed like this!"

Eleanor whispered, "Just think – we might be closer to finding this treasure than anybody
else before."

"We're just going to take photos of it, remember? We're not going to take it home and spend it."

"I know. But it's still exciting."

Vegas handed the phone to Eleanor and walked to the food trailer to get their food. She brought it to the picnic table and they began chowing down.

"This is so good," said Eleanor. "I wonder if they cater."

"I'm guessing if they do, August isn't going to bring it in his chicken outfit."

"The phone is about dead," observed Eleanor. "I'll need to charge it when we get back to our room."

Vegas took another bite of chicken. "This is so good. It's nice and crispy. August can fix some mean chicken."

"They didn't skimp on the serving size, did they?"

"It's the chicken platter, not the diet platter."

Eleanor tried to drink her milkshake, and she had to suck extra hard to get any flow going through the straw.

"Don't hurt yourself," said Vegas.

Eleanor took a gasp of air as if she had been deep-sea diving. "That's a thick shake."

Vegas looked absently at the road but noticed the large silver truck drive by. She quickly shouted, "Come on!"

"Come on what?"

"Come on, ma'am!"

"No. I mean where are we going and why?"

"We're going to follow that truck!"

They quickly gathered up their order, and Vegas raced into the driver's seat and slammed the door shut.

"Um, I have to come in this way," Eleanor said. Vegas quickly got out of the vehicle, and her mother crawled to the passenger seat and spilled the chicken on the floor. Vegas hurried back in, started the engine and killed it immediately, then got it going and took off in the direction of the truck.

"Who do you think is in this truck?" Eleanor asked before trying to get more shake out of the straw.

"I have no idea, but it's time we find out."

Vegas tried to catch up to the truck, but when they came to a long straightaway, it had disappeared.

"It's gone," observed Eleanor.

"How could it be gone so quickly? Oh, yeah, I know – it took us forever to get out of the parking lot."

"That's not on me."

"We can get to a lot of places quicker if you hadn't messed up my passenger side door. And now my interior smells like Big Chicken."

"The door isn't my fault."

"Yes, it is."

Eleanor thought about it. "Okay, I guess it is. But it's easily fixed. I think. If all else fails, you can just buy another door."

"Or I could just tie you up at your house so you would stop following me."

They were both quiet for a few seconds until Eleanor asked, "Well, what do we do now?"

"We go back to the motel, get some rest, then head out in the morning looking for Horses and Problems Ranch in Flat Bottom, Georgia, and see how the number three fits in."

"So you're not tying me up?"

"I didn't say that."

CHAPTER 13

VEGAS UNLOCKED THE MOTEL DOOR, then rammed her shoulder into it several times before it finally separated from the doorframe. As it did, her Diet Coke slipped out of her hand and fell onto the floor, spilling all over the red carpet.

"Oh, no!" shouted Vegas.

"What is it?" asked Eleanor, who was carrying what was left of their Big Chicken goodies.

"I dropped my drink and spilled it everywhere," Vegas said as she bent down and picked up the cup.

"They won't notice it," Eleanor said as she shut the door behind her. "You can have some of my milkshake, providing you can suck it out of the straw. That might be the thickest milkshake on the planet. It gave me a headache."

"No thanks," Vegas said. She threw her empty cup in the trash and got some paper towels from the bathroom to dry the carpet. After a bit, she stood up and stared at the wet spot as if it was an art project that didn't turn out right. "That's the best I can do."

"I'm sure that Spider-Man will approve. Are you going to take a shower?"

"I guess, unless you want to take one first."

"No, I'll let you go first. We need to check for cameras, though."

"What do you mean?"

"It's what all single attractive women like us should do when we check into a motel. We don't know anything about the motel owners." She then whispered, "Plus there's that little treasure thing we're looking for, too. We're prime candidates for cameras."

"I don't think Lazy would do something like that – setting up camera equipment to spy on your guests goes against her name."

Eleanor walked into the bathroom, turned on the light, and ran her hands over the walls looking for cameras. Satisfied that there weren't any hidden cameras on the walls, she turned to her daughter and asked, "Can you help me take the mirror down?"

"I'm not going to help you take the mirror down. Anybody that wants to see me naked deserves all the pain they get. Now, I'm going to take a shower and go to bed."

"Okay. If you need me, holler."

"I've not needed you at bath time for quite some time now."

"You never know."

Vegas locked the door after her mother left. She stared up at the ceiling, exasperated. "God, why did you make my mother so strange?"

"I can hear you," came back Eleanor's muffled voice.

"I wasn't trying to keep my thoughts a secret."

Vegas took the coldest shower she had ever taken in her life. She soon got out and got dressed in her Bugs Bunny pajamas.

"That was freezing," Vegas said, rubbing her arms in an attempt to generate some body heat. "We need to start a fire."

Eleanor looked around. "There's no fireplace in here."

"Then set me on fire," Vegas suggested as she climbed under the covers to warm up.

Eleanor stood up. "I guess I'll go take my shower now."

"You better make it fast, or icicles will grow on your nose."

Eleanor looked unconcerned. "I once went to summer camp when I was a little girl and they had a cold shower. It didn't bother me at all. In fact, all the other girls called me Doctor Freeze because I could handle the cold shower so well. They also called me Lady Marshmallows because I ate twenty-three at the campfire."

"Your superpowers are endless."

Eleanor went into the bathroom and turned on the shower. A few minutes later, she rushed out of the bathroom as if she was being chased by a pirate. She was wearing plaid-colored pajamas with a thick layer of green facial cold cream coating her face. She quickly got into bed.

"That was cold," Eleanor said, shivering.

"I thought you said that you could handle cold showers."

"That apparently was a long time ago," replied Eleanor. "I didn't even know water could get that cold. I tried to turn the hot water on, but nothing happened except more cold water."

"Well, we'll just call this a bonding experience and go to sleep."

"I like that. We don't bond enough."

"I think we bond too much."

"All daughters think that. Mothers think the opposite. When you have a daughter, you'll understand why I am the way I am about you."

Vegas stared at her mother's green face. "I've got to ask you a question."

"Let her rip! After all, that's part of the bonding experience."

"Why are you turning into the Incredible Hulk?"

Eleanor laughed. "Oh, this is my face cream that I got at the Dixie Discount a few weeks ago. It's supposed to give me a youthful glow. I think it works, too. I glow a lot now. It's almost like I'm a lightning bug in reverse." Eleanor started laughing. "Instead of my bottom glowing, it's my face."

Vegas smiled and yawned. "I'm turning off the light now. We'll get our rest, then try to find Horses and Problems 3 tomorrow."

Vegas turned off the lamp on the end table. It was quiet for all of two seconds when Eleanor shouted, "I forgot to charge my phone."

Vegas turned the light on as Eleanor got out of bed and opened her suitcase.

"The phone is over here," Vegas said and pointed at the end table.

"But my charger is in my suitcase. At least, I think it's in my suitcase. I sure hope I brought it with me. I wonder if I left it at home. We'll have to go back and get it if I did. I hope it's not there, or our whole vacation will be ruined."

"We aren't going back home to get a charger, and for the hundredth time, we're not on vacation! I'm on an investigation. If you don't have a charger, then we can buy one around here."

"That seems wasteful, since I have a perfectly good charger at home."

"The key words to that sentence are *at home.*"

"But it still works."

"I'm not saying it doesn't work. I'm saying that it isn't here. Besides, I'm sure you can always use a spare charger."

"What would I do with it?"

"In case you left one at home."

Eleanor thought it over. "Oh, that does make sense."

Eleanor continued rifling through her suitcase, then after a moment shouted, "Mommy found it!"

"Hooray," Vegas said unenthusiastically.

Eleanor walked to the end table and reached down to plug the charger into the wall. She stood up and hit the lamp with her head, knocking it off the table and onto Vegas' head.

"Mom, what are you doing?"

"Sorry, baby. Mommy's head got stuck in the lampshade when I stood up. But the phone's charging."

Eleanor picked up the lamp and crawled over Vegas to get back into bed.

"Mom, we aren't in the Volkswagen now. You don't have to crawl over the driver's side of the bed."

"Sorry."

"Are you done now?"

Eleanor began rubbing the covers smooth. "Mommy's done."

"Good night, woman."

"Good night, baby. Mommy loves you."

Vegas turned off the lamp.

A few seconds passed, then the television turned on. Its dim light slowly grew brighter, and the loud sound of the Atlanta nightly news filled the small motel room.

"What are you doing?" Vegas asked as she pulled the covers over her head.

"Mommy's watching TV."

"Would you turn it down?"

"I'm trying. There it is. I was pushing the button that doesn't do anything. Usually at home I push a button on my remote that makes the TV go to the menu, and I have a dickens of a time trying to get it off. Why is that, you reckon?"

Vegas pulled the covers off her head and glared at her

green-faced mother. "Mom, why are you watching television anyway?"

"This is what I do at night at home. It's part of the old woman routine that is done all around the world."

"But you're not at home."

"That's true. But I have a TV, so I thought I should watch it. I can put the mute on so there's no sound," informed Eleanor as she pushed a button on the remote and the menu came up. "What did I do now?"

"Give me the remote," Vegas said. She pointed it at the television and got the menu off. "You can watch thirty minutes of TV, then you have to go to sleep. I have a case to solve, remember?"

"Of course, I remember. I'm not dumb. I'm just a little bored."

Vegas rolled over and put the blanket over her head as Eleanor scrolled through the channels with the sound barely above a whisper.

"Hey, *Psycho* is on," Eleanor whispered excitedly.

Vegas threw the cover off her head. "I've got my own mother problems. I don't want to watch somebody else's." She then pulled the cover back over her head.

"Your father loved this movie. I didn't think much of it, because it scared me to death. The only reason I watched it was so I could hold your father. He was quite a man."

"I don't want to know what you and Dad did in your alone time," Vegas said in a voice muffled by the blanket.

"Well, let me tell you, our alone time was fun," Eleanor said with a wicked laugh. She turned back to the TV and yanked the blanket off of Vegas' head. "You'll like this part. It's where the detective is going into the house."

"I'm not interested."

"But maybe you can learn some tips for your case."

"He's not a real detective. He's an actor playing a detective. I'm a real detective."

"Like me."

"You're not a real detective either."

"Then what am I?"

"Don't tempt me."

They both watched as the old woman rushed out of a room with a knife and stabbed the detective, causing him to fall down the stairs. Eleanor quickly turned off the TV.

In the dark, Eleanor whispered, "I forgot that's what happened."

Vegas said, "It's a signal for me to stay away from other people's mothers."

"At least you didn't say that you wanted to stay away from your mother."

"That's apparently impossible."

CHAPTER 14

AT THREE IN THE MORNING, Vegas woke up. It took her a few seconds to get her bearings, but her mother's snoring helped her get her orientation.

A sound lightly filtered in from outside. Vegas listened intently, trying to decipher what it was. At first, it sounded like a child crying in a nearby room. Then she remembered that the other rooms were closed. But the more she listened to it, the more it sounded like a baby crying.

Suddenly Eleanor's green face popped up. "I hear a ghost!"

Vegas jumped in fright. "Ahh!" She calmed down and whispered, "You just scared me to death."

"Do you hear a ghost?" asked Eleanor as she hugged her daughter. "I don't want it to eat us."

"I don't think it's a ghost, and nothing is going to eat you with your scary makeup on."

"I knew I shouldn't have watched *Psycho*. I always have scary dreams afterward."

"Mom, you're not dreaming."

"That's what makes it even scarier."

They both listened carefully to the sound.

"Did I bring a cat?" asked Eleanor.

"No, you didn't bring a cat."

"I hear a cat."

"It could be a cat. At first, I thought it was a baby crying."

"I wish you'd get married and have a baby, and then I could come over all the time and babysit."

"You come over all the time now."

"I'm practicing."

Vegas walked to the window and peaked out the blinds. Eleanor asked, "What do you see?"

Suddenly headlights shone into Vegas' eyes, and she quickly ducked down. When the lights passed, she slowly rose up and looked out. She could see a large vehicle driving to the office.

"It's that truck again," whispered Vegas.

Eleanor made her way to the window and looked out. She pressed the left side of her face against the glass to try and see the office better.

"It *is* that truck. And I just got my facial cream all over the window," whispered Eleanor. "I wonder why they keep following us."

"I'm not sure. But they can see the Volkswagen right here. Why don't they come where we are?"

Eleanor turned around in a panic. "I don't want them over here. These aren't my good pajamas. These have a hole in the knee."

"I really don't think a hole in your pajamas is a big deal right now," whispered Vegas as she looked back out the window toward the office. "Eww, I got that green gunk on my face."

"It's not going to hurt you any," said Eleanor. "I think it's even edible." Eleanor took her finger and wiped the cold cream off of her daughter's face and dabbed it on the tip of her tongue. "I think I was wrong about it being edible," Eleanor said with a disgusted look on her face.

"I need to try and figure out why they're following us. I'm going out there," Vegas said.

Eleanor grabbed Vegas and hugged her. "I don't want you fighting whoever is in that truck." She pulled back and said, "If anybody is going to fight them, it's going to be me."

"Will you be quiet about fighting?"

"You brought it up."

"I didn't bring up fighting, you did."

"You said you were going to go out there."

"I'm not going to fight anybody. I'm going to get the license plate number and call Pepper to see if he can find out who it belongs to."

"Are you sure this will work?"

"No."

Vegas put on her shoes and headed to the door.

"Aren't you going to put on some clothes first?" asked Eleanor.

"Pajamas are your clothes at three o'clock in the morning."

Vegas walked out into the warm air of the darkness. She hurried to the back of the truck, hunched over to try and keep from being seen from anybody in the office. There was just enough light to make out the license plate: JBC-9066.

She began repeating the number in her mind. She then looked over the truck bed at the office. Lazy was talking to two men. She watched them for a few seconds, and then noticed a light in her room turning on and off. Vegas quickly made her way back to the room.

She opened the door and saw Eleanor with the lamp in her hands, turning it on and off. Vegas hastily closed the door and asked, "What are you doing?"

"I was turning the lamp on and off so you would know which room to come back to."

"I know which room to come back to. It's the one with the crazy green lady in it."

"Did you get the license plate number?"

"Yeah, JBC-9066. I need a pen."

Eleanor went to her purse and began searching through it for a pen. "I know I have one here somewhere. Hey, I got a spoon in here. I wonder what I put it in here for."

"Focus, Mom," Vegas said, repeating the license number in a whisper.

"I'm glad you remembered the license plate number because I could never remember that. I'd end up with BR-549."

"Don't put more numbers and letters in my mind," Vegas said. She grabbed her mother's phone.

"I found the pen," Eleanor said, holding it up like a prize ribbon from the county fair. "I wonder if it writes ... It's working! What was the number? BR ..."

"No, Mom, it's JBC-9066."

Eleanor wrote the number on her hand. "I got it! I hope it washes off later."

Vegas punched in a number on her mother's phone.

"Who are you calling?" asked Eleanor.

"Pepper."

"But it's three in the morning."

"He's probably up."

The phone rang three times before it went to voicemail. "This is Pepper. I'm not here right now because I'm out in the woods looking for the Wood Booger. Please leave your name and number and I'll get back to you unless I get killed by the Wood Booger or lost in the woods. Hmm, maybe I shouldn't have gone."

Vegas ended the call. "He's still out Wood Boogering."

"Do I erase the number on my hand then?"

"No," Vegas said. She tapped the phone against her forehead, trying to think of what to do.

Eleanor went to the window and looked out. "What should we do now? Hey, I could write some sort of note on the side of their truck door. I mean, I did find the pen."

"Yeah, that makes a lot of sense to write on the side of a truck that's been following us. Now stop looking out – they might see you."

"I can't help it. You act like the people in this truck are going to kill us, so that makes me want to look."

"I'll call Sergeant Miller," Vegas said. The phone rang three times, four times, five times, six times. ...

Then a deep voice came over the line. "What?"

"You don't sound happy," said Vegas.

"I'm never happy at this time in the morning. Who is this?"

"Vegas Chantly."

"Tell him I said hi," Eleanor said.

"Mom, he doesn't care if you say hi or not."

"Do you know what time it is?" asked Sergeant Miller.

"Why wouldn't I know what time it is?" asked Vegas.

Eleanor placed her hand in her daughter's face. "Here's the license plate number."

Vegas pulled her hand down. "You could just tell it to me."

"What do you want?" shouted Sergeant Miller.

"I'm in a motel just outside of Atlanta, and I believe a truck is following us. The license plate number is–"

Eleanor shouted, "JBC-9066, JBC-9066, JBC-9066!"

"JBC-9066. That's good, Mom. You can have a snack now."

"Why are you telling me this?" asked Sergeant Miller.

"I want you to look it up and see who owns the truck. They've been following us."

"Who are us?"

"They're following me and my mom."

"Why are they following you?"

"I'm on a case."

"I'm not part of your security team."

"But I need to know who it is."

There was a sigh. "Let me get a pen and paper."

Vegas could hear clanking and banging as Sergeant Miller looked for a pen and paper.

"What's taking so long?" asked Eleanor.

"He's looking for a pen and paper."

"He can have mine," Eleanor said and offered her pen to Vegas.

"I don't think he can reach it from where he is, Mom."

Eleanor shouted into the phone, "Write it on your hand like I did! Do you think he heard me?"

"People in Des Moines heard you," said Vegas.

There was a loud thud from Sergeant Miller's end.

"What happened?" asked Vegas.

"What happened?" asked Eleanor.

"I don't know. Hello?"

"I got a pen and paper," Sergeant Miller said.

"What was that noise?"

"I fell out of bed reaching for the pen and paper."

"I'm sorry."

"What happened?" asked Eleanor.

"He fell out of bed."

"Maybe he should get a hospital bed that has a rail on the sides. Your cousin Mary works at an online company that sells hospital equipment. I have the number somewhere in my purse. Here, let me talk to him," Eleanor said, reaching for the phone.

Vegas turned away from her. "Mom, would you go sit down?"

"Would you two stop fighting so I can go back to sleep!" pleaded Sergeant Miller.

"I think we all know that we'll never stop fighting."

"Just give me the license plate number," Sergeant Miller said in a desperate voice.

"It's—"

"JBC-9066!" Eleanor shouted as she looked at her hand.

"JBC-

"I heard your mother. Now go away."

There was some groaning on the line, and they heard Sergeant Miller speak to his wife. "Honey, you're going to have to help me back up."

Vegas ended the call.

"Is he going to look it up for us?" asked Eleanor.

"Yeah, as soon as his wife helps him off of the floor. Listen, maybe we should head out now."

"Now? It's three in the morning."

"But it might not be safe here," Vegas said. She walked to the window and saw the truck leaving the parking lot.

"I think we should wait and leave when the sun comes up," suggested Eleanor.

"Well, maybe that's best. Driving these Georgia back roads at night probably isn't the best thing for me or my Volkswagen."

"What time do you want to get up?" asked Eleanor. "Seven?"

"Seven is fine."

"Deal," Eleanor said and spit in her hand and held it for Vegas to shake.

"I don't think that's necessary."

"Come on. It's the universal bond of seven-year-olds everywhere."

Vegas shook her mother's hand. She then looked at her hand. "I've got ink on me."

"We're bonding now."

CHAPTER 15

VEGAS' eyes slowly opened, and the small motel room came into focus. She sat up rubbing her eyes, and then checked the time on the cellphone. It was just before seven o'clock. She sat back against the headboard and looked at the window blinds. She could see the rising sun peeking in. Then she noticed the sound she had heard in the night. It was definitely some sort of cry, she thought. She turned to her mother to ask if she heard it, but Eleanor wasn't there.

"Mom?" There was no answer.

Vegas got out of bed and headed toward the bathroom. The door was closed and she knocked on it. "Mom, are you in there?" There wasn't an answer. Vegas opened the door. Not there either. Panic was beginning to rise in her chest, and she quickly went to the room door and threw it open.

"Mom?"

Vegas checked inside the Volkswagen, but her mother wasn't there. She turned to her right, where to her surprise, she saw her green-faced mother on her knees with her right arm inside the exit slot of the Pepsi machine.

Vegas walked over to her. "Mom, what are you doing?"

"There is a cat up in this pop machine, and I'm trying to get it out."

"A cat?"

"Yes. That's what we've been hearing. I wonder what its name is."

"A cat being where it isn't supposed to be sounds like an Eleanor to me. You're not stuck there, too, are you?"

"No. At least I don't think I am," Eleanor replied.

"How long have you been out here with your arm shoved inside a pop machine?"

"I'm not really sure. I woke up and couldn't get back to sleep. I may have eaten too much chicken, or it could have been that milkshake froze something in me that isn't supposed to be frozen, but I couldn't get to sleep. What time is it now, anyway?"

"Seven."

"That's funny. Time flies when you have your arm up a pop machine. I came out here about five."

Vegas was shocked. "You've been out here for two hours? Why would it take two hours to do anything?"

"I had to get this kitten. At least I'm pretty sure it's a kitten. A cat would be too big to fit up here. I'd hate to pull out a groundhog or a possum. That would be a vacation memory, wouldn't it! Wait a minute ... I think I've got it," Eleanor said and slowly pulled a kitten out of the machine and hugged it to her chest. Its white fur was matted and tangled. It meowed constantly as Eleanor hugged it.

"That looks like one tired kitten," observed Vegas.

"I'm going to call it Pepsi. We need to feed it something. Do we have any chicken left from last night?"

"We've got enough chicken left to start a bunch of problems. Listen, we need to go get dressed, then head on out of here."

"Okay. I better get Pepsi something to drink, too. I wonder how long he's been in there."

The three of them went into the room and got ready to leave. Vegas went to the office to check out and found Lazy sitting in a chair reading a newspaper.

"Hello," said Vegas. "We're checking out. Here's the key."

Lazy stood up, folded her newspaper, and placed it on the counter. "Okay. Did you two sleep well last night?"

"I did okay considering I was with my mother."

"I don't mean to pry, but does your mother have a drinking problem?"

"No, she just acts like it. Say, who was that in the big truck around three o'clock this morning?"

Lazy suddenly looked uncomfortable. "I'm afraid I don't know what you're talking about."

"It was a big truck with big tires. I believe it was silver. I thought they had checked in."

"We get people that pull into the parking lot all the time that are just trying to get cellphone service. That's probably all it was."

"So they didn't come into the office and talk to you?"

"No."

"Are you sure?"

Lazy glanced away, and then looked at Vegas. "What concern is it of yours?"

"I was just curious. Well, I'm off to my next grand adventure."

"Where are you heading?"

Vegas was surprised she asked the question, but she had no intention of telling her. "Whichever way the wind is blowing."

Lazy looked out the window and said, "The wind doesn't appear to be blowing right now."

"That could complicate things."

The two of them stared at each other for a moment, trying to figure out what the other was hiding.

Lazy broke the silence. "Are you heading north?"

Eleanor suddenly appeared holding the kitten in her hand. "We're going to Flat Bottom, Georgia."

Vegas looked at her mother, horrified.

"What's in Flat Bottom, Georgia?" asked Lazy.

Eleanor looked at her daughter and realized she shouldn't have said that and tried to rectify the situation as best as she could. "We're going to see Uncle Nat's turkey farm. Yeah, that's it. He has turkey rides there for the kids."

Vegas began to wonder if her mother actually did drink.

"Well, we need to head to Uncle Nat's," Vegas said and ushered her mother out the door.

"Have a great day," replied Lazy.

As they walked to the Volkswagen, Vegas asked her mother, "Why did you tell her where we were going?"

"It slipped out, but luckily I recovered with my Uncle Nat story."

"I don't think turkey rides count as recovering."

"I thought it was best to try and use confusion as a tactic."

"I didn't know if you were trying to confuse her or me. Now, what are you going to do with that cat?"

"Technically it's a kitten, and I'm going to keep it."

"You can't take it with us."

"Sure I can. It needs a home, and I'm going to give it one. I'm a mother, so that type of thing is built into my system. When you become a mother you'll understand better."

"So you're a cat lady now?"

"We all become cat ladies eventually."

Vegas shook her head. How would she be able to advance her case with a cat and a crazy woman with her?

Her mother brought her out of her thoughts when she accidentally honked the horn on the Volkswagen while crawling over the seat. "Sorry!"

Vegas got in the car and watched as Pepsi climbed on Eleanor's shoulder.

"He seems all better now," Eleanor said. "He ate all that chicken and drank enough water to fill several cat-sized swimming pools." She laughed but noticed her daughter's look of concern. "What's wrong?"

"I asked Lazy about that truck that came in last night. If she knew who they were."

"What did she say?"

"She said there was no truck and she didn't talk to anyone."

"That's not true. I saw the truck. I think I saw it. Did I see it?"

"Yes, you saw it, Mom. When I went to get the license plate number, I saw two men in the office talking to her. Why would she lie about that?"

"Maybe she's seeing one of them behind the other's back. Doesn't sound like she's as lazy as we were being led to believe," Eleanor said with a nod.

"There was no reason for her to lie about them to me unless she's somehow in on it with them."

Eleanor hugged her kitten. "In on what, honey?"

"I'm not sure. They're following us for some reason, and I have to think it's about the treasure. There's no other reason for them to be following us."

"So they're trying to follow us so when we find the treasure they can take it from us?"

Vegas stared at her mother intently. "Well, they're not *trying* to follow, since you told them where we were going."

"So she didn't believe my story about Uncle Nat?" Eleanor said.

"Nobody believed the story about Uncle Nat."

"So I should have used a different name from Uncle Nat so it would have been more believable?"

"I think it was the turkey rides for the kids that got you off the rails."

"I'll keep that in mind the next time I have to cause confusion."

Vegas wondered at what age her mother had been dropped on her head.

"Let's just go, Trouble," said Vegas.

"The kitten's name is Pepsi."

"I wasn't talking to the kitten."

CHAPTER 16

ELEANOR SEARCHED the maps on her phone for Flat Bottom, Georgia, while Vegas tried to drive. It was proving difficult, as Pepsi kept getting in the way.

"Why is that cat climbing around everywhere?" asked Vegas.

"It's been in a soda machine for some time now, so this is like a grand hotel of some kind to him. Let him stretch his legs, he needs to exercise. And speaking of which, I started back on my Zumba class."

Vegas glanced at her in surprise. "I thought you always dreaded going to that."

"Not anymore. It's all about attitude."

"I agree that you have attitude."

"Afterward, some of the girls and I go to the pizza place next door. It's kind of like our reward for a hard workout. It was my idea," Eleanor said with a smile.

"I'm not surprised it was your idea, but doesn't going out for pizza sort of negate all the exercise you do beforehand?"

"It balances out, I say. We had a pizza eating contest the last time. I had six slices."

"Why would you eat six slices of pizza?"

"Because I wanted to win," Eleanor said matter-of-factly.

Pepsi began playing with Vegas' hair. "Mom, your cat is trying to do my hair!"

"It's about time somebody did."

"And his claws are going to ruin my interior."

"It wasn't that great to start with."

Annoyed, Vegas changed the subject. "Have you found Flat Bottom yet?"

"Yes. Turn in one mile. On the right. You take Route 55."

"Route 55 on the right, got it."

"What should we do to make some vacation memories?"

"For the one-thousandth time, it's not a vacation!"

"Maybe we could tell some jokes."

"I'm not in the mood for jokes, Mom."

"I've got a few jokes about unemployed people, but none of them work," said Eleanor. She started laughing at her own joke.

"That's terrible, Mom," Vegas said, but she couldn't help but laugh, too.

The Vokswagen crossed a long iron bridge that looked like something out of a horror movie. Eleanor took note of its name. "Bad Creek Bridge. Now that's an interesting name for a bridge."

"I guess they had to call it something," said Vegas, who noticed Pepsi hanging on Eleanor's seat back. "What is that cat doing now?"

Eleanor unbuckled her seat belt, turned around and sat in the seat on her knees to look at the cat. "It looks like he's defying gravity. We have a super cat of some sort here. I wonder if he can talk, too. Say, 'I'm Pepsi.' You can do it. I'm Eleanor. Don't say that part. I was just introducing myself."

"Stop confusing the cat, Mom. And since you own him, he'll never be able to get a word in edgewise."

"That doesn't seem like a nice thing to say to your mother," said Eleanor as she twisted her way back around in her seat and started trying to fasten her seat belt.

"You tore up my door. The cat is tearing up my interior. You two definitely belong together."

"I can't get the seat belt to give me any slack."

"You tore up my seat belt, too?"

Eleanor pulled on the seat belt as if she was trying to start a lawn mower. The belt finally gave some slack, but she accidentally hit the steering wheel, which caused Vegas to swerve left and overcorrect to the right.

Vegas pulled over as soon as she could.

"Why did you do that?" asked Vegas breathlessly.

Eleanor said, "I had to fix the seat belt. Mission accomplished, by the way."

"This is the worst vacation ever," mumbled Vegas.

Eleanor pointed at the road sign outside the passenger side window. "Oh look, we're at our turning road. Route 47."

"I thought we were looking for Route 55."

Eleanor looked at her map. "You're right. Forward ho!"

Vegas got back on the road and followed it until she saw the Route 55 sign. "There it is."

"We're like truckers or cab drivers," said Eleanor. "It's like we're made to travel like this. Oh, we should do this for our next vacation. We could go on a road trip. Maybe we could rent a bigger vehicle, though. Like one of those RVs. Oh, that would be fantastic!"

"I can't drive an RV."

"Your husband can drive it for us."

"Oh, yeah, my future husband driving me and my mother around in an RV shouldn't cause us any marital problems," Vegas said sarcastically.

Vegas noticed an abandoned ranch on the right. She

stopped in the entrance of the driveway. "This might be it here. Look at the mailbox. Does it have a name?"

Eleanor attempted to roll down the window, but it wouldn't budge. "The window isn't rolling down."

"Can't you see through it?"

"It's dirty. You really need to give it a bath. I have some soap back home that I wash my vehicle with that works wonders. It is as shiny as can be. It's so clean, you can eat off of it. Of course, if I set the food on the hood, I wouldn't be able to reach it. I wish I knew where my step ladder was. Mommy might not be tall, but her vehicle sure is pretty."

"Just tell me the name on the mailbox, woman!"

Eleanor stared out the window at the side of the mailbox. "It's hard to make out because the lettering is so faded. It looks like P-E-A-B-O-O- wait, did I already say O?"

"Are you saying there are two Os, or are you stuttering?"

"No, there's just one O. I have to start again. P-E-A-B-O-D-Y. What's that spell?"

"Peabody. This is the right place."

The two of them looked over the obviously abandoned ranch house. It had a large horse barn to the right with broken fencing and fields that had grown over with grass and scattered saplings.

"This is a lot like the place I grew up in," said Eleanor.

"Well, it doesn't look like anyone has been growing up here for some time now."

"What do we do now?"

"We go and see if we can figure out what Horses and Problems 3 means."

"We can't just drive on the property and walk around. That's trespassing."

"There's nobody here. We shouldn't get into too much trouble," said Vegas.

"Are you sure this is the place?"

"There's a sign laying down up here. I'll see what it says."

Vegas drove up the drive a little farther and got out. Eleanor started climbing over the seats to get out of the driver's side when she got hung up on the gearshift lever.

"Vegas, Mommy's hung up."

Vegas ignored her mother and looked at the sign lying beside the driveway. At one time, it had hung above the driveway, she noticed. She knelt down and rubbed away the dirt and grime and revealed the words *Horses and Problems Ranch*.

"This is it," Vegas said and turned toward the vehicle and saw her mother's feet hanging out of the driver's side door. She quickly made her way to her.

"Vegas, Mommy's stuck!"

"How did you get stuck in the driver's side floorboard?"

"I don't know. I must have blacked out or something. Or maybe time travel was involved somehow."

"There is no such thing as time travel," said Vegas as she reached in and got her mother's pant leg cuff off of the gearshift lever. Eleanor slid out onto the ground like she was on a child's slide. "Are you okay?"

"I've not been okay since you got ol' Yellow here."

Vegas helped her mother up. "Are you sure you're okay?"

"I'm fine. I think."

"That's not very reassuring. I'm going to drive up the driveway. Get back in the vehicle."

"But I just got out."

"Well, you have to just get back in. Now scoot."

"But I just got out!"

"I heard you the first time. Remember, I didn't tell you to get out."

"Getting in and out of this vehicle is kind of like a vehicle Zumba class. Hey, maybe I can start that."

"Just get in."

Eleanor crawled back in without incident, and Vegas drove up the steep driveway to the ranch on the hill and parked.

"I hope this emergency brake holds," Vegas said as she pulled the brake.

"I'm sure it will."

"It should hold as long as you don't kick it while trying to get out."

"I'll not kick it."

"I'll help you out. I can't wait to get that door fixed so you'll stop climbing over everything like Spider-Man's mother."

"I don't think Spider-Man had a mother," Eleanor said.

"Lucky him," Vegas mumbled and helped her mother get out.

"See, I didn't hit anything," Eleanor said and threw her hand up to stress her point and hit the door. "That doesn't count."

Vegas sighed. "Let's just look around."

"What exactly are we looking for?"

"For the number three. Can't you leave the cat in the vehicle?"

"You can't leave your child in a vehicle."

"It's a cat, not a child."

"Vegas, he'll hear you," Eleanor whispered and covered the cat's ears with her hand.

"Whatever," Vegas said. She walked to the house's front porch and looked about. Eleanor walked beside her and set Pepsi on the ground.

"I bet this was a nice-looking house at one time," observed Eleanor.

"I'm sure it was," Vegas said as she peered inside the windows.

"Do you see anything?"

"No. All the rooms are empty. I wonder what the number three represents."

"Maybe its three calling birds like in that Christmas song."

"I doubt that," responded Vegas. She made her way to the third window on the right and looked through it. There was nothing more than what appeared to be an empty bedroom. She walked back to the front door and walked around three windows to the left and looked inside and saw the dining room. There was nothing that represented a clue in her eyes.

Vegas turned around to talk to her mother but didn't see her. "Where did she go now? Mom? Where are you?"

Her mother peeked out from around the corner to the house. "I lost Pepsi."

"Would you just forget the cat?"

"I can't forget the cat, Vegas. It's a living creature that's had a hard life."

"Living with you isn't going to make its life any easier."

Eleanor disappeared around the corner of the house and Vegas followed. Once around the corner, she didn't see her mother anywhere.

Vegas hurried to the stable and found her mother with Pepsi in her arms.

"I found him! He must have come into the stable here because he wanted to play horsey. Mommy will play horsey with you when we get back home, I promise."

"You are distracting me from the task at hand."

"What task?"

"What do you mean what task? We're looking for Horses and Problems 3."

"We're at Horses and Problems."

Vegas glanced at the stalls and noticed that they were numbered one to six. She walked to number three.

"It's got to be the stalls! This has to be the three it's talking about."

Eleanor smiled. "Pepsi helped you find it. Hooray for Pepsi," she said while holding the cat's left paw up in celebratory fashion.

Vegas slid the stall door open and walked inside. She looked about but didn't see anything that seemed like a clue.

"Do you think it could be buried under the ground here?" asked Vegas as she looked at the dirt floor.

"If it is, then how deep could it be?"

"I don't know," Vegas said and looked up. She noticed some sort of engraving on a wooden plank in the ceiling.

"What are you looking at?" asked Eleanor.

"Something is engraved on that board up there. Do you see a ladder anywhere?"

Vegas and Eleanor looked about the barn and found a ladder propped against a wall. Vegas carried it over and positioned it under the engraving. When she could reach the ceiling, she wiped the plank off with her hand so she could see it clearly.

"Is it anything?" asked Eleanor.

"It's definitely an engraving."

"I cut your father's name into a tree with a pocketknife when we first started dating. I went back the next day and a beaver had cut it down. I was afraid that was a warning for our relationship, but it wasn't. Just that we had a beaver problem."

"The beaver was probably warning me. ... I think I can make this out. It says, 'The Troll Lives Beneath The Bridge Where The Water Is Bad.'"

Eleanor looked puzzled. "That doesn't make sense. Trolls aren't real, are they?"

"No," Vegas said and wrote the phrase in her pocket notebook. "But maybe the clue is."

Vegas climbed down the ladder and stood beside her mother as she stared at her notepad trying to decipher the clue's meaning.

"Maybe that's not the clue," suggested Eleanor. "Maybe that's just something some kid wrote, and the clue is somewhere else in here."

"It's in stall three – this has to be it. Give me your phone so I can take some pictures with it."

"Gotcha," Eleanor said. She set her purse on the ground and rummaged through it like a kid opening Christmas presents.

"Why can't you keep track of that thing?"

Eleanor pulled out her phone from her purse. "I found it! I knew I would, I just didn't know when."

Vegas took the phone and climbed back up the ladder to take pictures. She then climbed back down and got the coordinates from Google Maps and wrote that down in her notebook, too. She then handed the phone to her mother.

"I'll put it beside the can of nuts I have in here. That way it should be easier to keep track of. Oh, did you want some nuts?"

Vegas didn't answer, as she saw two men walk by outside. Eleanor noticed Vegas' eyes enlarge as if she had seen a ghost or current meat prices.

"What's wrong?"

"There are two men outside," Vegas whispered.

"Are they the owners of the place?" asked Eleanor.

"I don't know," Vegas whispered. She quietly walked to the window. She could see her Volkswagen on the steep driveway, and behind it was the large silver Ford F-550 that had been following them.

"It's that truck!" Vegas whispered. "We have to get out of here."

Vegas grabbed her mother's hand, and they ran for the

Volkswagen. They got to the vehicle, but the truck was close behind them, and the driveway was too narrow for them to drive around without possibly getting stuck over the hill on either side.

"How do we get out of here?" asked Eleanor.

"You get in the vehicle, and I'll take care of the truck."

"Okay. Pepsi says to be careful."

Vegas looked at the cat, which had its paws on the edge of Eleanor's purse like a child riding in a little red wagon. She shook her head and walked to the truck. She looked in and saw it was a manual. She tested the door and found it open, and quietly got in.

On the dash was some sort of monitor. It had a grid on the screen and a red flashing light. Were they tracking them? Vegas wondered.

She noticed the emergency brake was on. She shifted the truck out of gear and got out beside the truck. She then released the emergency brake, and the truck rolled backward just enough so the Volkswagen could pass.

Vegas turned around and was surprised to see her mother standing there.

"What are you doing here?" Vegas whispered loudly. "I told you to get in the car."

"Pepsi had to go to the bathroom, but he's done now. I guess it's from all the excitement. Or it could be from the chicken."

"You took him to the bathroom now?"

"When you gotta go, you gotta go."

"Well, we gotta go."

"You can go behind the vehicle if you want."

"Just get in the car. We have to get out of here."

"Okay, okay."

The two of them ran to the Volkswagen and Eleanor got in as quickly as she could. Vegas saw the men walking around.

"They're coming!" Vegas shouted as quietly as possible. "Hurry up!"

Vegas saw one of the men pointing at them, and she instantly felt panic rush through her body.

Eleanor whispered, "I think my purse strap is hung up on some—"

But before Eleanor could get the rest of the word out of her mouth, Vegas shoved her into the passenger seat, started the vehicle, and began backing up, her mother's butt against the side of her head.

The two men were running now, but Vegas drove away just before they could be caught.

"Did we escape?" Eleanor asked from the floorboard.

"I'm going to have to get that door fixed," Vegas said.

CHAPTER 17

VEGAS DROVE AS FAST as her Volkswagen could go, which was exactly fifty-one miles per hour. She kept looking in her driver's side mirror, fearing the truck would come up on them at any moment.

Eleanor, meanwhile, was still positioning herself in the passenger's seat, and Pepsi sat in the back playing with some Christmas decorations that he found underneath the driver's seat.

"Are you okay?" Vegas asked.

"I was until you pushed me into the floor," she said as she fixed her hair and straightened her clothes.

"We had to get out of there. This is why I don't want you coming with me on these cases.

It's too dangerous. We have this conversation every time, and you never listen to me. You just go ahead and break into my life anyway."

"Don't worry about me. I can take care of myself. Remember my Zumba class?"

"If a pizza eating contest ever takes place on one of my cases, then we're good. Other than that, you need to stay home."

"How did those men find us, anyway?" Eleanor asked, trying to change the subject.

"The only way they would have known which direction we had gone is if Lazy told them."

"How would she know that?"

"Because *you* told her!" shouted a frustrated Vegas.

At that moment the Volkswagen began to sputter. Vegas looked at their speed, which was slowly dropping.

"What's wrong?" Eleanor asked.

"I don't believe this!" shouted an angry Vegas.

"What?"

Vegas saw a gravel road on the left and maneuvered the Volkswagen toward it. The car came to a stop, and Vegas just shook her head.

"What's wrong?" Eleanor asked again.

"We're out of gas," Vegas whispered and began drumming her fingers in irritation on the steering wheel as if she was waiting for her order at a slow restaurant.

Eleanor looked at the fuel gauge, pushing Vegas aside. "How can we be out of gas?" Eleanor said.

"You just run out."

"Are you sure we're out? It looks like there's some left."

"That's just your angle. The needle says empty. It's the only thing left on the car that you haven't broken."

They were quiet for a few seconds when Eleanor said, "We need to stay positive."

Vegas rested her head on the steering wheel and said, "I was going to get gas this morning, but I forgot. I was thinking about Lazy lying to me and about those men being at the motel last night, then I got to thinking about the clue Horses and Problems 3 and wondering what that could be, then there was the cat in the pop machine, and then you. There is always you."

Eleanor replied, "You know, something just occurred to

me. We've met a person named Lazy and a cat named Pepsi. That's rather amazing, isn't it?"

Vegas slowly turned her head toward her mother while the side of her face still rested on the steering wheel. "We're out of gas being chased by men for God knows what, and the most amazing things are the names Lazy and Pepsi?"

"They're very peculiar names, and we met them in the same place. What are the odds of that happening? Pretty slim, I'd say," Eleanor said and crossed her arms for emphasis.

"You do know that you named the cat?"

"Technically, the pop machine named the cat. Now, what are we going to do?"

Vegas leaned back in her seat and thought over the situation. "Your cellphone, give me your cellphone. Where is it?"

"It's in my purse. But who are you going to call?"

"Just get me your phone and we'll go from there."

Eleanor looked around the vehicle. "Where is my purse? Here pursey, pursey, pursey. I had it on my seat until somebody shoved me and then – oh, look, Pepsi found some Christmas decorations. Isn't he adorable? Look at your brother, Vegas."

"He's not my brother."

Eleanor took the decorations from Pepsi and placed them around her daughter's neck. "You look like the cutest thing ever. If you were a Christmas tree, I'd buy you without thinking twice."

"The phone, mother," Vegas said sternly.

Eleanor frowned. "Obviously *this* Christmas tree is going in the corner."

"Just give me the phone, Mom."

"Okay, okay," Eleanor said. She turned around to face the back, got on her knees, and searched the floor in back. "Here's my purse! I knew it was here. Man, you must have pushed me hard. Stop kissing Mommy, Pepsi."

Eleanor sat down properly in her seat, purse in hand. "It's a good thing I wore my flexible pants today. If I wore my blue jeans, I would not have been able to bend over like that and reach my purse. We'd be calling the gas man and a seamstress," she said with a hearty laugh.

Eleanor began searching for her phone. "Everything got unorganized when I ended up upside down. Of course, I guess that always happens when a body gets turned upside down. Oh, here it is."

Eleanor gave Vegas the phone, and she took it and got out of the vehicle. She walked around holding the phone in the air, looking like the Statue of Liberty casting spells.

"I'm not getting a signal anywhere here," Vegas said.

Eleanor crawled out of the driver's side with Pepsi in her hands and lost her balance. "Vegas, help Mommy up."

Vegas hurried to help her mother. "Why did you get out of the vehicle?"

"I didn't see any reason to stay in there since we don't have any gas. How are we going to get some, anyway? I don't even know how far we are from a gas station."

"I know," Vegas said with a sigh. "Do we even have anything that will hold gas?"

"I'm pretty good at holding gas. I ate way too much cereal the other morning, and I was as gassy as I've ever been. I didn't know cereal would do that to a person. Tony Tiger and I are going to have to have a talk."

Vegas went to the rear of the vehicle and opened it up to see the engine compartment. She slammed it shut in frustration. "I keep forgetting the stupid trunk is in the front."

"What are you looking for?"

"Something to put some gas in," Vegas said and opened the real trunk. "There's nothing here to hold gas." She slammed the trunk shut.

Suddenly they both heard a noise from the highway. They knew it had to be the truck that had been following them.

"That's them coming," said Vegas. "We have to hide."

Vegas grabbed her mother by the hand and led her and Pepsi into the woods. Vegas came upon a large rock, and she instructed her mother to hide behind it. From their spot, they saw that the truck didn't stop; apparently it hadn't seen the Volkswagen through the trees it was halfway hidden behind.

"That was close," Vegas said. She noticed her mother staring straight ahead. "What's wrong?"

"Something over there is moving," Eleanor whispered and pointed.

Vegas looked in the direction her mother was pointing but only saw a bush. Then she saw movement.

"It's moving," Eleanor whispered.

Vegas got up and whispered back, "I saw it, too."

"What is it?"

"Maybe it's just the wind."

"The wind isn't blowing," observed Eleanor. "I'll prove it." Eleanor wet her index finger and placed it into the air. "This is how you can tell which way the wind is blowing. The cool side of your finger means the wind is blowing from the right side. Or is it the warm side of your finger that you're supposed to pay attention to? Well, I don't feel anything, other than my finger being wet."

Vegas stared at her mother. "Thank you, Weather Channel. I believe we're just on edge because of the guys in that truck. I wish I knew who they were."

"What do we do about the bush creature?"

"It's not a creature. It's just a bush blowing in the wind, or maybe there's a squirrel or a bird in it moving around giving it that horror vibe."

"Should we throw rocks at it?" asked Eleanor.

"What, why?"

"So it doesn't come over here and eat us."

"If someone threw rocks at me, I'd definitely come over."

Eleanor wouldn't stop staring at the bush in dread, so Vegas walked up to it. "See, it's just a bush, Mom. There's nothing to worry about."

The bush rustled again, and Eleanor yelled, "It's the bush monster!"

Vegas ran back to her mother, and they hugged each other in fright. After a moment, they heard a voice.

"Hello."

"Did the monster just talk?" asked Eleanor.

"I believe it did."

The voice called out again. "I'm sorry I frightened you. I'll not harm you in any way, I assure you."

The bush moved forward and a suit of some sort was pulled off, revealing a skinny middle-aged man with a small black mustache. "Hi. I'm Toby Joe."

Vegas and Eleanor stared at Toby Joe, unsure of how to react.

"I'm sorry for frightening the two of you," Toby Joe said with a look of concern on his face. "I've been out on patrol today."

Vegas finally found her tongue. "What are you patrolling?"

"Wood Boogers. I'm in the Georgia Wood Booger Club, and this week we're out in full force throughout the state to try and find them."

Relief crossed Vegas' face. "I think my friend Pepper is in your club."

"Oh, that's fantastic. Are you all out here looking for a Wood Booger, too?"

"No. We're looking for gas," said Eleanor.

"You mean like a natural gas line? I saw one back east

there. Do you all work for the gas company? Nice cat, by the way."

"His name is Pepsi," informed Eleanor.

"That's an interesting name. Does he do any tricks?"

"Oh, cats don't do anything you tell them," Eleanor said with a hearty laugh.

"Yeah, they're like mothers," added Vegas.

Eleanor shot a disapproving glance at Vegas and said, "He does walk on the ceiling of vehicles."

"That's nice," said Toby Joe.

"What exactly are you wearing there?" Eleanor asked.

"This is my gullies suit. It makes me invisible in the woods so that when a Wood Booger walks by, I can take photos of it."

"Have you seen one?"

"Not yet. But I've smelled them around here."

"Smelled?" Vegas asked.

"They give off a terrible stench. If you smell one, you'll have no doubt what it is. Well, it could be a dead skunk, but other than that, it's more than likely a Wood Booger. Do you all want to join my search? I'd be happy to have you. I've got my campsite just over the ridge here. It's not far at all."

"Thank you for your offer, but my vehicle ran out of gas. Do you know of a gas station around here?"

"I've got gas I can give you. I always bring twenty gallons of gas when I go on my Wood Booger patrols because you never know what might happen."

"We should start doing that," suggested Eleanor.

"Where am I going to store that much gas in a Volkswagen?"

"In your trunk – if you can remember which end of the vehicle it's on."

"You collect Volkswagens?" asked Toby Joe.

"I don't collect them, I just drive one."

"I have ten back at my house. I work on them and fix them up and such. Of course, most of them don't run. I guess I'm not the best mechanic in town. But I like Volkswagens. Did you know they were built by the guy that created Porsches? I can't remember what his name was ..."

"I think it was Porsche," said Vegas.

Toby Joe said, "No, that was the name of the car. Well, anyway, I love Volkswagens. I have a book about them back at the campsite even. It tells their history, if you're interested. It gets boring sometimes looking for Wood Boogers. Don't tell the club I said that."

"Let's get back to the gas," Vegas said.

"Do you need some gas?" asked Toby Joe.

Vegas was confused by his question, as they had already discussed this, but she reminded him again. "Yes. We ran out. We'll pay for the gas."

"Oh, that's not necessary. I'm a full believer that if you help someone in need, then it will come back around when you need help. Sort of like karma."

"That's almost poetic," said Eleanor.

"I saw it in a TV ad for paint."

"Well, just as long as you try to help. Sometimes when you try to help, people get mad at you," Eleanor said, looking at Vegas.

Vegas replied, "Especially when they mess up your car door while trying to help you when they weren't supposed to be coming along in the first place."

There was an uncomfortable silence between the three of them for a few seconds. Then Toby Joe said, "Why don't I go get that gas so you all will leave."

CHAPTER 18

TOBY JOE EMPTIED his can of gasoline into the fuel tank of the Volkswagen. "That should be enough fuel to get you to the gas station," he said.

"Which way is the gas station?" Vegas asked.

"You have two choices. Go west here and you'll find a convenience store that has the best coffee in Georgia."

"I don't know if we should go west," Eleanor said as she snuggled Pepsi. "That's the way those men went."

"What men?" Toby Joe said.

"It's nothing," said Vegas.

"Is somebody following you? I know karate, and I'm pretty good at throwing rocks." Toby Joe got into his karate stance and moved his hands in a circular motion in front of him, then above his head, almost knocking off his hat.

Vegas looked at Toby Joe. He was in poor physical shape, and she didn't see much hope of his being able to help them fight two large men. "We'll be okay."

Toby Joe said, "Well, there's another gas station east of here. It's not as nice as the other. And the coffee isn't as good, but they do have beaver cake. Have you all ever eaten that before?"

"No," Eleanor and Vegas said in unison.

"It's a delicacy. That's what I use on my Wood Booger hunts. Wood Boogers love beaver cake. At least that's what the cashier at the store told me."

"Is it made from beavers?" asked Vegas.

Toby Joe pondered the question for a moment. "You know, I never asked."

Vegas decided it was time to leave. "I really thank you for the gas."

"It's no trouble."

"I don't know what we would have done if you hadn't shown up," she said.

"We would have died," Eleanor said.

"We wouldn't have died," Vegas said. "We would have argued, but not died."

"You have to know how to survive out here in the woods," said Toby Joe. "You never know what might happen. Some survivalists even drink their own urine to survive."

"I don't think that I'd ever get that thirsty," Vegas said.

"Could you do something like that?" asked Eleanor.

"I've never done it before," replied Toby Joe. "I don't even know what position you get in."

The three of them stood silently for a few seconds.

"Well, I'd never drink my own urine," said Eleanor. "Do they sell it in stores?"

"Just buy the water, Mom. Now let's go," Vegas said, opening the driver's side door. Eleanor and Pepsi crawled in, and they headed east toward the store that sold beaver cake.

"He seemed nice," Eleanor said.

"He seemed odd."

"I'm sure we seemed odd to him, too."

"One of us did anyway."

"You know, without him we would still be there wondering what to do. God is protecting us."

"I just wish he would use normal people to help us."

They had driven three miles when they saw a sign that read, "Best Beaver Cake in Georgia!" It was scrawled in red paint on a piece of plywood propped against a power pole at the gas station.

Vegas got out and her mother called to her, "Vegas, here's my credit card for gas."

"I don't want to use your credit card."

"But you don't have any money."

"Argh," Vegas said under her breath. She reluctantly took the credit card and used it to pay. As she filled up the tank, Eleanor crawled out, leaving Pepsi to roam about the Volkswagen interior.

"Where are you going?" asked Vegas.

"I just want to look around. I thought I might get a snack and some cat food for Pepsi.

He seems hungry. You seem hungry, too. Do you want anything?"

"I'm fine."

"You look hungry. You never eat enough. You're nothing but skin and bones now. I'll get you something. It's a good thing I'm with you or you'd starve to death," Eleanor said.

"Don't cause any problems."

"I'm not going to cause any problems," Eleanor said as she walked in front of a moving vehicle that was pulling in next to the gas pumps on the other side of where the Volkswagen was refueling. "Sorry," she said with a wave and went inside the store.

Two boys got out of the vehicle that almost hit Eleanor. They were talking loudly.

One boy said, "I can't believe I lost my balloon at that bridge."

The other boy responded, "Why did you let go of it?"

"I didn't, the wind blew it out of my hand. I think the bridge was bad luck."

"Any bridge called 'Bad Creek Bridge' is bound to be bad luck."

Those words slammed into Vegas. She reached into her pocket and pulled out her notebook to read what she had written down from the barn earlier today. "The troll lives beneath the bridge where the water is bad."

It had to be Bad Creek Bridge, she thought. She was putting the clues together when the gas pump shut off with a clank and startled her. Vegas quickly put the nozzle up and went inside the store to get her mother.

She found her mother eating cake while talking to several people. She laughed through a mouthful of cake. Vegas walked to her.

"What are you doing?" she whispered.

"I'm eating beaver cake, and it is absolutely delicious! That plywood sign they have out front wasn't lying. Of course, plywood signs rarely do. I wonder why that is? It tastes just like real cake. Do you want to try some?"

"No. We have to go."

"I got some cat food for Pepsi. It's called Star Cat Food. I think that sounds good. If I was a cat, I think I'd eat it. I got ten cans. Oh, my goodness, I have to get a can opener. It's a good thing I said that out loud just now or I would have forgotten to get the can opener, and Pepsi would not have been pleased with Mommy," Eleanor said. The other people gathered around stared blankly at her. "Do you want something to eat or drink?" Eleanor asked Vegas as she walked to find the can openers.

"We don't have time for that. I want to go."

"I got you something. A few candy bars and a Coke. Gee, I hope buying a Coke doesn't cause a conflict with Pepsi. Maybe the cat won't notice. I'm not sure. Cats are strange people."

"So are mothers. Let's go."

Eleanor found a can opener and paid for her things. "Your alls sign was right – this is the best beaver cake in Georgia!" she said to the clerk. Vegas pulled her by the arm out of the store.

"What's your hurry?" asked Eleanor.

"I know where the next clue is."

"Where?"

"I'll tell you on the way," Vegas said and pushed her mother toward the Volkswagen.

"You never give me any respect," said Eleanor.

"What do you mean?"

"You won't tell me anything."

"I do give you respect. Now crawl in."

CHAPTER 19

AS VEGAS DROVE the Volkswagen back toward the Bad Creek Bridge, Eleanor warned her, "This is the direction those men went. Are you sure we should be going this way? I don't want to run into them again. I'm not made for quick getaways."

"It's where the next clue is, so I don't have a choice."

Eleanor was quiet for a few seconds before she asked, "Where are we going?"

"Remember the clue?"

"The clue? Yeah, the clue." Eleanor thought about it for a moment and then asked, "The clue about what?"

"That's what we've been doing here these past few days," Vegas said in frustration as she watched Pepsi crawl on the ceiling of the Volkswagen. "We're trying to figure out the clues to get us to the treasure."

It all came back to Eleanor. "Yeah, yeah, it was Horses and Problems 5."

Vegas shook her head. "It was Horses and Problems 3. But that's not the clue we're looking for now."

"Horses and Problems wasn't a clue? Then what were we doing in that barn? Mercy sakes, we were at the wrong place," said Eleanor in a bit of a tizzy.

"It was a previous clue, Mom. The clue we're looking for now is, 'The troll lives beneath the bridge where the water is bad.' It was on the plank in the barn."

"So you believe there's a troll living beneath a bridge?"

"No."

"Then why are we going to wherever it is where we're going?"

Frustration filled Vegas' face and she sighed. "Listen. Do you remember going over the bridge with the name Bad Creek Bridge?"

Eleanor arched her eyebrow, trying to remember it.

"Never mind," said Vegas. "We passed over that bridge, and that has to be where the troll is. It hit me when I overheard two boys back at the store when I was pumping gas. They mentioned Bad Creek Bridge where one of them lost their balloon."

"Well, that's sad," Eleanor said with a pouty face. "Did his parents buy him another one?"

"I don't know."

"I would have bought him one if I knew he lost it."

"You need to stay focused here," Vegas scolded.

"It's hard to stay focused when you learn that a little boy lost his balloon and I could have bought him another one and didn't. I feel terrible. I also feel full of beaver cake."

If Vegas hadn't been driving she would have banged her head on the steering wheel. But after a few quick breaths she tried again.

"We're going to Bad Creek Bridge and look under it."

"Is that safe?"

"I don't know. It could be muddy under there. Might be a lot of water, or it could be dry. It hasn't rained in awhile, so maybe it won't be too bad."

"That's not what I'm talking about," said Eleanor. "I mean what if there's a troll under there?"

"There's no such thing as trolls."

"Then why did the clue mention a troll?"

"I don't know. We'll just have to figure it out when we get there."

Eleanor looked ahead and pointed. "Isn't that the bridge up there?"

"Yeah, that's it."

Vegas drove slowly toward the bridge as she looked for a place to park. With no parking spot on the north side of the bridge, she continued to the south side. Eleanor looked down at the water and observed, "It doesn't look very deep at all."

"That's good. I can park here."

Vegas parked the car on the right side of the road near a barbed-wire fence. She got out, then assisted her mother and Pepsi out of the vehicle, then handed the cat back to its adoptive mother. Vegas began to look for a way down below the bridge.

Eleanor stopped. "I forgot my purse. I'll be right back. Oh, hold your brother."

Vegas took Pepsi. "We're going under a bridge. You don't need your purse."

"My phone is in it. I want to take a picture of the troll."

"Just get the phone out then."

"A woman needs her purse with her at all times. It's a lifeline. You should know this by now."

Eleanor ran back to the vehicle with a slight wobble, opened the door, and got her purse. She closed the door but caught the strap of her purse in it. She opened the door back up, freed the purse, and then headed back toward Vegas and Pepsi.

"I made it," Eleanor said, trying to catch her breath.

"Are you going to be okay?"

"I will once my head stops spinning. I don't think my Zumba class is working."

"Maybe it's the pizza afterward that's causing your problem," suggested Vegas. She handed the cat to Eleanor, who placed him inside her purse with his head sticking out so he could see the troll.

They walked toward the end of the bridge. There wasn't a way down beside the bridge, but some woods were on the upstream side of it. They were able to walk through them and circle back to beneath the bridge. The water was about two feet deep and flowing gently. There were sand dunes on both sides of the water beneath the bridge next to the supports.

"Which side will our clue be on?" asked Eleanor.

"I'm not sure. I wish I didn't break my shovel. I need something to dig with."

Vegas looked underneath the bridge to see if there was a clue like back at the barn, but nothing revealed itself. Vegas looked on the ground and found a piece of eighteen-inch rebar. She began digging with it.

"What are you doing?" asked Eleanor.

"I'm digging for trolls."

"Did you ever think when you became a private investigator that one day you would be looking for trolls?"

"Not at the beginning. But now it doesn't surprise me at all."

Vegas got on her hands and knees and dug around. She found cans, plastic sheets, sticks, rocks, and just about everything else that wasn't a troll.

Eventually Vegas stopped digging and sat down to think. "This could be anywhere, and I don't even know what exactly I'm looking for."

"I thought it was a troll," Eleanor said and took Pepsi out of her purse to let him play.

"But what shape is it? Is it a drawing on the pier or a buried statue? If it was under here, it could have been washed away by a flood or covered by all this dirt and sand several feet deep."

At that moment, Pepsi walked to the edge of the water and began pawing at a leaf. The leaf released from the bank and Pepsi reached out for it and fell in the creek.

"My baby!" shouted Eleanor. Vegas turned and saw her cat brother struggling to get to the bank on the far side of the creek.

Eleanor ran into the water to rescue Pepsi and fell almost immediately and began splashing around. "Help me! I'm drowning!"

Vegas jumped in the water and grabbed hold of her mother's arm. "Just stand up!"

Eleanor stopped thrashing and stood up with help from Vegas. "I forgot it wasn't that deep. But when you fall in water under a bridge, the first thing you think about is drowning. Well, actually the first thing you think about is why did I come down here under this bridge? Where's Pepsi?"

They both looked across the way and saw that Pepsi was on the bank trying to dry off by shaking himself. Vegas took Eleanor's arm and they waded to the far bank. Eleanor scooped up Pepsi and held his face against hers. "You gave Mommy quite a fright there! I'm glad you're okay."

Eleanor snuggled Pepsi and plopped down on the wet creek edge. Vegas stood in the water watching her mother and the cat, wondering how she would dry off.

"I'm going to have to change clothes," Vegas said.

"You'll dry out," said Eleanor.

"I shouldn't have to dry out."

"I'm sorry, but I thought I was drowning."

"Now you know how I feel every day of my life when I find out you're coming over."

"What's that supposed to mean?"

As the women argued, Pepsi walked to the bridge abutment and began digging around. After a moment, he uncovered the edge of a box and meowed at it.

"What's he meowing about?" asked Vegas.

"He probably found a ball or something. Cats like balls because of their action nature."

Vegas saw the corner of what appeared to be a wooden box and immediately headed toward it. She dropped to her knees and began digging around it.

"What did you find, Pepsi?" Eleanor asked as she scooped him into her arms. "Is that what we're looking for?"

"I'm not sure, but I'm going to find out. I need something to dig with other than my hands."

Vegas looked about and realized she had dropped her rebar in the water when she was helping her mother up. She walked back in the shallow water, retrieved her rebar, went back to the box, and began digging.

It took several minutes, but eventually she was able to wiggle it out of the ground. It was a pine box about four inches wide and seven inches long. She looked it over and found a latch on one side. She opened it and inside found a garden troll statue.

"This is it! This is the troll we're supposed to find!"

"Pepsi found a troll!" Eleanor said excitedly. "Most cats just hunt mice, but Pepsi solves riddles like a superhero. Mommy will have to buy you a cape and get you a little mask to wear. That would be so adorable."

Vegas picked up the troll and turned it every which way in her hands.

"What are you doing?" asked Eleanor.

"I don't see any clue here. I just see a troll in a box. I don't know what the next clue is."

"Maybe it's in the box."

Vegas sat the troll down and looked in the box. She saw some faint words written on the lid. "There's definitely something written down here, but I can't make it out. Maybe if I could shine a light on it or something. Let's get out of here and see if we can figure it out later. I don't want to run into those men in that truck again."

"I thought we were just supposed to take pictures of it and put it back."

"I have to figure it out first. We'll just take it up to the vehicle and look it over, then I'll bring it back."

"Pepsi and I agree with that. Maybe we can get another motel room tonight. That was fun. Maybe we can even find another cat for Pepsi to play with."

"We aren't adding to the band. Now, let's go."

They headed back to the Volkswagen, Vegas examining the troll and the box the entire walk. "I still can't make out the writing on this box."

"Maybe it says, 'Rub my tummy and I'll grant you three wishes,'" Eleanor said with a laugh.

Vegas rolled her eyes. Then something caught her eye.

"We've got a flat tire," Vegas said dejectedly. She walked to the rear of the vehicle and examined the tire.

"A flat tire? How did it go flat?"

"I guess I ran over something here on the side of the road or maybe back at the barn. Now I've got to change it."

"Do you know how to change a tire?"

"I helped Dad change the tire one time. I learned a lot about the English language that day. We took it off and it rolled down the hill."

"The tire or the vehicle?" asked Eleanor.

"Both, actually."

Vegas walked to the front of the vehicle and opened the trunk. She placed the troll back in its box and set it in the trunk and grabbed the jack. Before she could do anything else, the large silver truck pulled in behind the Volkswagen. Vegas, Eleanor, and their superhero cat had no place to go.

CHAPTER 20

TWO MEN – one tall and skinny, and the other short and chunky – got out of the truck and walked toward them. Vegas' fear turned to anger as she blurted out, "Who are you?"

The men stopped in their tracks, and the tall one said, "I'm Skunk, and this is Squirrel."

Vegas and Eleanor looked at each other as if they had walked in on the last part of the movie and didn't understand what was going on.

"We just keep adding to our interesting name list on this vacation," observed Eleanor.

"Mom, for the hundredth time this is not a vacation."

Eleanor looked at the animal men and said, "I'm Eleanor and this is my daughter Vegas and our cat Pepsi."

Vegas turned to her mother. "Don't tell them who we are."

"They told us their names."

"I'm guessing they didn't."

Skunk said, "We didn't mean to scare you two."

"Why have you been following us?" Vegas asked angrily.

"Well, it really wasn't real following," Skunk said in what sounded like an unsure voice.

"No," said Vegas sternly. "It *was* real following. I want to know why you were following us and I want to know now."

"Yeah," said Eleanor, trying to sound tough. "Or we'll put your knuckles in the blender."

"Blender?" Vegas said.

"It was the first thing that came to my mind. Should I say we're going to bite them?"

"We're not putting two men named after animals in our mouths," Vegas said as she stared at the two men.

Skunk tried to explain things. "See, me and Squirrel, he's my older brother by two years–"

"We were almost twins," interrupted Squirrel.

Skunk ignored his brother's comment. "We're members of the Riddles and Riches Society. We've been going to all their meetings, except during hunting season, and word has gotten out that there was this hot chick solving some of the riddles."

"Two hot chicks," interrupted Eleanor.

Skunk continued. "So we were following you all to get help with the clues."

"There's a Riddles and Riches Society that's based on this puzzle?" asked Vegas.

"Sure is," said Skunk. "Me and Squirrel here were the founding members. We were going to have membership cards and stuff, but that was too complicated, and neither one of us can spell that good anyway."

"I love clubs," Eleanor said. "I was in 4-H in high school. We went to the county fair one year, and some of the others talked me into riding a cow. It was a great club, though I was banned from future field trips."

Vegas placed her right hand on her forehead and sighed. "I'm dealing with too much strangeness at the moment."

"Maybe you should lie down," suggested Eleanor. "You've been working a lot lately."

"You can lie down in our truck," Skunk said.

"Why don't you do that?" urged Eleanor.

"I'm not getting in a stranger's truck."

"They're not strangers anymore," Eleanor said. "We're all in the same club."

"That's right," Skunk said.

"Hold everything!" shouted Vegas. "Let's start at the beginning here. First, I don't like people following me, no matter what their club affiliations are. Also, I'm working for a client, and I'm not going to give you any information that I have found. You would have to ask my client for that information."

"What's your client's name?" asked Skunk.

"I can't give you that information unless said client gives me permission to let you know their name."

"Are you talking about Mr. Harper or us?" Eleanor asked in a whisper.

"Be quiet, Mom," Vegas whispered back.

"We saw you all come up from under the bridge," Skunk said. "Did you find a clue down there?"

Vegas quickly tried to think of a reason to be down there. "Uh ... my mother had to go to the bathroom."

Squirrel looked at the two women, who were soaked from the creek. "She sure did."

Skunk tried to get them back on track. "Listen, I know it doesn't look none too good to have us following you around, but we've been stumped by this puzzle for some time. Everybody in the whole society has. When word got out that somebody was actually solving the clues, we just had to know some of the answers. So me and Squirrel put our heads together and–"

"You would think they would put their tails together with names like Skunk and Squirrel," Eleanor whispered to Vegas.

"We can hear you, ma'am," Squirrel said.

"Sorry," Eleanor said. "It's just that sometimes I think out loud."

"And sometimes she just talks out loud," said Vegas.

Squirrel continued. "What we're proposing here is that we team up. You know, like the Justice League or X-Men or, well, I guess you can pick your own superhero team."

"That sounds like fun," Eleanor said to Vegas. "I'd love to make a costume and dress up. We'll go by the name Jumbeliah Sisters."

"I don't team up with people I don't know, and to be honest, I don't trust you two," Vegas said, ignoring her mother.

"We're the Snodgrass brothers," said Skunk.

"Squirrel and Skunk Snodgrass," mused Eleanor. "Kind of an 'S' thing going on there, isn't it?"

"They're just nicknames, but we've been called Skunk and Squirrel for so long we up and forgot our real names," said Squirrel.

"My daughter's not married."

Vegas stared at her mother in humiliation. "Mom, why are you telling them that?"

"I tell everybody that you're not married. It's my way of trying to get word out that I want you to get married."

"We're not married either," Skunk said.

"You might want to consider a name change," said Eleanor.

"We like to play the field," Squirrel said and hitched up the front of his pants for emphasis.

Skunk added, "But the field don't like us."

Squirrel nodded in agreement, and as he did so, he noticed the flat tire on the Volkswagen and informed Vegas of the obvious. "You got a flat tire there, ma'am."

"I know."

"Well, Skunk can change it for you," Squirrel said. "He used to work as a mechanic until he burnt the garage down."

"They fired me after that, but I understood."

"Do you have a spare tire?" asked Squirrel.

"Yes," said Vegas.

"We'll put it on for you," said Squirrel as he and his brother approached the Volkswagen.

But then it dawned on Vegas that the troll was in the trunk next to the spare tire. She didn't want them to know about it and quickly came up with a plan.

"You can't open that!" shouted Vegas.

"Does the latch not work?" asked Squirrel.

"No, that's the door," said Eleanor.

Squirrel said, "I got a hammer in the truck. We'll get it open for you."

"No, it's not that," said Vegas. "The trunk, um, is where I keep my unmentionables. A lady can't have two gentlemen seeing her unmentionables."

Skunk and Squirrel blushed and Squirrel said, "I'm sorry, ma'am. I didn't mean to put your unmentionables onto the gawking post."

Eleanor whispered to her daughter, "What are you talking about?"

"Never mind," Vegas whispered back.

"Wait a minute, is unmentionables a code word for something?" whispered Eleanor. "Are we supposed to rush them?"

"No," Vegas whispered to her mother. She then addressed Skunk and Squirrel: "My mother and I will get the spare tire out."

Vegas and Eleanor - and Pepsi - walked to the trunk of the Volkswagen.

"What in the world are you talking about?" whispered Eleanor.

"I don't want them to see the troll," whispered Vegas.

"But it's in a box. They can't see it."

"But it looks like a coffin, which is suspicious. I don't want them asking any questions."

"So you don't trust them?"

"I don't trust anybody," Vegas said as she unscrewed the wing nut from the tire carrier, then pulled the spare tire up and out of the vehicle. Vegas grabbed the jack and hoisted it out of the vehicle and closed the trunk.

"I got it out for you all," she said.

Skunk grabbed the spare tire and Squirrel took the jack. "We'll have this fixed for you in no time, but me and Skunk were talking over there, and we'd like to run something by you."

"Run something by me?" Vegas asked, now on guard.

"Yeah," Squirrel continued. "We're meeting up with someone this evening about the Riddles and Riches clues, and they said they can help us. I thought maybe we could include you all on the deal to sort of make up for scaring you all by following you."

Vegas thought it over a moment. She wasn't sure taking them up on their offer was a good idea. "Who is this person you're meeting?"

"We can't tell you right yet because we have to ask them if you two can come with us or not," said Squirrel.

"She won't mind," Skunk said.

"I don't think she will either," added Squirrel. "She likes hanging out with people. Though you all might want to change into some dry clothes first."

"We'll be there and we'll be dry," Eleanor said.

"You don't get to decide this," Vegas said to her mother.

"I don't see why not. It helps everybody. We help our case and they help their obsession with the Riddles and Riches game, and we all get to meet new people, making for a fun vacation."

"We already know who she is," Skunk said.

"Okay, some of us get to meet new people," added Eleanor.

"Meet us tonight at nine o'clock behind the Lazy Susan Motel," Squirrel said. "Now we'll get this tire fixed for you."

Vegas watched the two men start working on her flat tire and then asked, "How come we have to wait until nine tonight?"

"That's when her powers are the strongest," Squirrel said.

Vegas shot her mother a look. Eleanor told her, "Sounds like we're going to meet a superhero."

"Or a vampire," Vegas added.

Squirrel and Skunk worked on changing the flat tire for about an hour because several of the nuts didn't want to budge. At one point, the two men took off their shirts. Vegas thought they were trying to seduce her with their imperfect bodies.

"We got her changed," Squirrel said. "I'm sorry I'm all hot and sweaty." Then for some reason, he flexed his bicep. Skunk saw him and flexed his as well.

Skunk said, "Did I mention neither one of us are married?"

"There are a lot of lucky women around here then," Vegas said with a fake smile. "Listen, I want to thank you two for changing my tire – and of course for the show – but we really need to get going now."

"I understand," Squirrel said. "Will I see you tonight?"

"Uh, no, I'm working on something tonight, so I'm not going to be able to come," said Vegas as she took the flat tire and jack and put it back in her trunk.

"Are you sure?" asked a disappointed Squirrel. "I really think if you come then we can advance to the next clue. I'm sure she knows what it is. She has the gift."

"Gift?" asked Vegas.

"I can't tell you anymore than that, but you'll never forget the experience," Squirrel said.

"Thank you, but I believe I'll pass. Do I owe the two of you anything for changing the tire? Moneywise that is."

"Oh, no. It was an honor to help out a pretty lady," Squirrel said, which made Skunk blush.

"Thank you," said Vegas, and shook both gentlemen's hands. She then got into the driver's side door but remembered her mother had to climb in and got out.

After they were on their way, Eleanor asked, "Why didn't you want to go to the meeting tonight?"

"Do you really believe those two guys have any idea what they're talking about?"

"I'm sure they know what they're talking about sometimes."

"I think I can do this myself."

"Nobody ever does anything by themselves," Eleanor said. "That's why they have mothers."

CHAPTER 21

THAT EVENING, Vegas pulled the Volkswagen into a parking lot overlooking a lake. Vegas got out with a bag of hamburgers and fries, and a drink holder. She held the driver's side door open with her knee for her mother, who crawled out with Pepsi in her arms and her backpack of a purse slung over her right shoulder.

They walked to a picnic table, and Vegas set down their dinner and headed back to the Volkswagen.

"Where are you going?" asked Eleanor.

"I'm going to get the troll."

"That's a good idea. He might want to see the lake. It's pretty here."

Vegas just shook her head and then retrieved the troll and its coffin-looking box from the trunk. When she got back to the picnic table, she saw Eleanor chowing down on a cheeseburger.

"Mom, that's my cheeseburger," Vegas said, sitting down.

"I thought they were the same thing."

"You ordered the monster burger," Vegas replied and showed it to her.

"Oh, yeah that's right. Well, you can have it."

"I can't eat all of that. It's the size of my head."

"I'll eat it then. You can have your cheeseburger back."

"You already ate a piece off my burger."

"I'm not poisonous, for crying out loud."

"I'll just eat the monster burger."

"You're a strange little girl, do you know that?"

"I wonder where I get that from," Vegas said and struggled to get her mouth around the large triple-stacked pieces of meat and bun.

Pepsi walked along the picnic table as Eleanor opened the box housing the troll. "I used to have something like this in the yard, but we called it a gnome. Are a gnome and a troll the same thing?"

"I don't know. They look the same to me. This is the largest hamburger in the world," Vegas added with frustration. "Here, Pepsi, help me eat this thing."

Vegas took two of the three hamburger patties and placed them on the table for Pepsi, who smelled them and walked away.

"Maybe he's not hungry," Eleanor said.

"Maybe he's wiser than me for trying to eat this thing."

Vegas set the burger down, took several drinks of her soda, and wiped her hands and mouth with a napkin provided by The Fun Bun. She reached over and grabbed the troll box, then took out the statue and stood it on the picnic table.

"I think we should call it Warby," said Eleanor.

"Warby? We're not supposed to name it."

"We weren't supposed to take it, either, but we did that. Seems like if we stole it we should at least name it," said Eleanor.

"We're going to put it back. I just can't figure the clue out on this one as easily as the other ones. I have to be missing something obvious here."

"I think Warby is a good troll name. I really want to keep it."

"No, Mom, we have to put it back and turn all our photos and coordinates over to my client."

"A client which you haven't taken the time to call," Eleanor said before taking a drink of her soda.

"I don't trust him. I feel like he's been keeping things away from me that would have helped me solve this. Maybe he doesn't want me to solve it."

"Now, why would that be?"

"Who knows."

"I think you're just getting a little paranoid. It doesn't make any sense to hire two private investigators to–"

Vegas stared at her mother. "He only hired one private investigator."

"Okay, I'm free."

"No, you cost quite a bit to have around."

Eleanor looked at her daughter disapprovingly and replied, "I don't cost that much. Besides, I think we should let him know what you found. It's the polite thing to do."

"Maybe you're right. I'll call him."

Eleanor dug inside her purse, and after several minutes of searching pulled out the cellphone and handed it to her daughter. Vegas looked through her notepad for Mr. Harper's phone number. She punched in the number and waited.

The call eventually went through, but there was a lot of background noise. She heard a clicking sound when Mr. Harper spoke.

"Hello?"

"Mr. Harper?"

"Yes."

"This is Vegas Chantly, your private investigator."

"Say again. It's very loud in here."

"It's Vegas Chantly, your private investigator. You hired me to look into the *Riddles and Riches* puzzle," Vegas said loudly.

"Why are you screaming?" asked Eleanor.

"He's in a crowded room and can't hear me."

Mr. Harper replied, "Oh, yes. What do you have for me?"

"I've found three clues so far. I'm now looking at number four here to try to figure out where the next one is."

There was a long pause, then a half-hearted, "That's great."

The loud sounds in the background irritated Vegas and she asked, "Where are you? I hear a lot of people around."

"I'm at the Bandit Casino in Bristol, Virginia. I'm having a blast, too."

"I see. Well, I just wanted to let you know about the status of the case."

"Sure. I thank you for helping me out here. I'm going to have to go now."

"What?"

"I said I'm going to have to go now."

Mr. Harper ended the call.

"He didn't seem to be very impressed that I was able to find these clues when nobody else has been able to. It was as if he already knew or something."

"Maybe he's not surprised that you're as good as you are," said Eleanor, patting her daughter on the shoulder in praise. "You get your detecting and keen observation from me. You're welcome, by the way."

"Thanks," Vegas said in an unbelieving voice. She began looking in the box that the troll came in to see if she had missed anything.

"What are you looking for in there?" A blob of ketchup fell

from Eleanor's burger onto her shirt, and she wiped it away with her napkin.

"I wish I could read the writing in here. I can't quite make it out because it's faded."

Vegas began angling the box in the sunlight in hopes the sun would hit the lettering just right and she could see what it said. After repositioning it several times, she was able to make out some words.

Vegas said the words aloud slowly and was able to figure out the partial words. "It's not what's on the outside that counts, but the inside."

"You can see that?" asked Eleanor, who tried to look into the box but had it pulled away by Vegas.

"Yeah, if you look at it in just the right light. But what does it mean? 'It's not what's on the outside that counts, but the inside.'"

"That's what mothers have been telling their children ever since children were invented. I'm sure I told you that several times in your life," Eleanor said with a mouth full of hamburger.

"But you didn't write it down and put it in a box with a troll."

"Maybe it would have had more impact if I had. I never really thought about it. I should have been more creative in giving you advice when you were little. I had that gnome I could have put something inspirational in. Like, 'Eat your vegetables' or something like that."

"If I found a note in a gnome that said eat your vegetables, I'd have thought it came from the devil and smashed it."

Vegas wrote the box's words in her pocket notebook. She read it over and over, then looked at the troll. She looked back at her notebook, then to the troll again. She whispered, "Smash the gnome."

"I heard you the first time, and I would not have been happy about that. That thing cost me seventeen dollars, and that was a lot of money back then."

"How would I have seen your 'eat your vegetables' note unless I got inside the gnome?"

Eleanor thought it over. "I guess that's true. Of course, I could have just put the note in his hand hole. See, when we got him, he held a metal ring that had the words 'hooray for gnomes' written on it. So I could have put the note in that. But it would have gotten wet in the rain because you'd probably take forever to find it. You weren't as observant when you were little as you are now. You came home one time with half your sandwich, and I asked you how come you didn't eat it all and you said you forgot. Why did you forget?"

Vegas abruptly stood up, lifted the troll over her head and smashed it hard onto the picnic table. As it broke into three large chunks, Eleanor shouted, "What in the world is happening here?"

Vegas pointed. Inside the troll was a piece of paper.

"If that says 'eat your vegetables,' I'm going to faint," said Eleanor.

Vegas picked up the piece of paper and read the typed message out loud. "Lazy Susan can provide you rest. At the Falcon Tree it knows best. In the bottle a clue does nest. It will take you to riches blessed."

"Lazy Susan?" questioned Eleanor. "Is it talking about the motel we stayed at?"

"It must be," Vegas replied.

"That's where Skunk and Squirrel are going. Or is it Squirrel and Skunk? I don't know which one is the leader."

"I'm pretty sure they're leaderless," Vegas said.

"Well, they invited us there tonight and you could have looked for the clue there, but you said no."

"I didn't know about the clue at the time. All I knew was that I didn't want to be around them any longer."

"We were supposed to take a picture of this gnome before you destroyed it. Now we're going to get into trouble," Eleanor said.

"I can still take the photos. It had to be done, though. The clue was inside. But what's a Falcon Tree?"

Eleanor took the note and read the poem again. "*Lazy Susan can provide you rest.*" Eleanor thought it over. "Now that's the motel. *At the Falcon Tree it knows best.* I don't know what that is."

"Look it up on your phone and see if there is such a thing," suggested Vegas.

Vegas took the note while Eleanor Googled Falcon Tree. "There doesn't seem to be anything called a Falcon Tree," Eleanor said. "Oh, look, here's a video of a little baby laughing! It's so cute. Do you want to see it?"

Vegas ignored her mother and read the next line of the poem. "*In the bottle a clue does nest.* What bottle?"

"Maybe it's buried at the base of the Falcon Tree."

"If there even is such a tree. *It will take you to riches blessed.* That means it's the last clue and will take you to the treasure. I just don't understand about the Falcon Tree."

"What you need to do is go to the motel and look around."

"I remember there were woods behind the motel and a hollow between the woods and the motel. But a Falcon Tree doesn't make any sense. Maybe it's what people around here call it."

"I bet Skunk and Squirrel would know."

"What makes you think that?"

"They changed our tire."

Vegas looked at her mother, confused. "What does that have to do with anything?"

"I don't know. It just seems to me if you can change a tire, you have to have some sort of knowledge in life."

"Well, I don't know how to get a hold of them."

"We'll call the Lazy Susan Motel and ask."

Vegas thought it over. "Lazy *was* talking to them, so she might be able to help us out. Get the phone number to the Lazy Susan Motel."

"Right, chief," Eleanor said with a salute.

Vegas shook her head. "We're the woman version of Skunk and Squirrel, aren't we?"

"Everybody has a Skunk and Squirrel in their family," Eleanor replied as she scrolled through her phone looking for the Lazy Susan Motel number. She found the number and handed the phone to Vegas.

"Lazy Susan Motel."

"Is this Lazy?" Vegas said.

"Yes. Is this about the spoons I ordered?"

"Uh, no, this is Vegas Chantly."

"Vegas Chantly? Oh, the one with the crazy mother?"

Vegas was startled by the comment. "I hate to be remembered that way."

"You'll need to leave her behind then."

"That apparently is impossible. Listen, I'm looking for Skunk and Squirrel. I don't know their real names–"

"Blain and Dwayne Snodgrass. They're idiots."

"We're talking about the same people then. How come when I asked you about the men in the truck you said you didn't know them?"

"Oh, right, I wasn't supposed to say that. Well, anyway, they're my cousins. I was afraid you were going to try and take advantage of them so I thought it best to protect them from you."

"I wouldn't do that. Do you know how I can get in contact with one of them?"

"They're here now. Skunk is picking his teeth and Squirrel is staring at me like he wants to talk to you. I think he likes you."

"Uh ... I just need to talk to one of them for a—"

Before Vegas could complete her sentence, a man's voice spoke. "This is Squirrel. What do you need? Is your tire okay? Is this business or personal?"

"It's business."

"Rats," said Squirrel.

"I was wondering if I could join you tonight for the meeting about the next clue."

"You sure can! I called her and she said she had some great information for us. We can make you a new member of the Riddle and Riches Society, too. I'll bring the gong."

"Gong?"

"It's part of the ceremony."

"I just wanted to try and find out the next clue. Do I have to become a member of the society for that?"

"I don't really know. We've never discussed it. We just thought everybody would love to be part of the club. I mean, it's a great society to be in. We have field trips looking for clues and such, then we go to the park and play tag."

"Is this woman that's going to be there part of the society?"

"She sure is. Is your mother coming?"

Vegas looked over at her mother, who looked at her anxiously. "When are we leaving?"

Vegas shook her head. "Yeah, she'll be there."

"I'm still going to bring the gong. I'll see you two tonight at nine o'clock sharp."

"Okay. See you then."

Vegas hung up the phone and handed it to her mother.

"You don't seem very excited," observed Eleanor as she dropped the phone into her purse.

"I feel like I'm accumulating too many strange people in my life."

Eleanor said, "Good thing I'm here to give you some calmness."

CHAPTER 22

VEGAS AND ELEANOR put the troll and its box back beneath the bridge after taking photos then recording the coordinates, and just before nine, they pulled into the Lazy Susan parking lot. Vegas turned off the Vokswagen and looked around.

"I don't see Skunk and Squirrel's truck anywhere."

"They must not be here yet. Uh-oh, do you think this is a setup and they're going to make us dig our own graves?"

"Mom, I highly doubt they're murderers. Besides, I'd refuse to do it."

Eleanor thought over the scenario. "I'll hit them with the shovel they give us."

"What if they make you dig it with your hands?"

"Then I'll pick up a handful of dirt and throw it in their faces and take off running."

"What about me?"

"If you hadn't refused to dig your grave, you'd have a handful of dirt so that you could throw at them."

"I don't have to throw dirt at them. I'll just have you talk to them and they'll eventually take off running. They'd be shouting, 'Make that woman stop!'" Vegas said while holding her hands to the sides of her mouth as if she was yelling loudly.

They both started laughing.

Just then, Lazy came out of the manager's office and gave them a hardy wave. She walked to the driver's side window, which Vegas had rolled down because of the heat. "Skunk and Squirrel just called, and they're on their way. They got held up by a bat that got into their mother's house."

"I hope everybody is all right," Vegas said.

"Everybody's fine but the bat. They were trying to wrap a towel around it while it was resting on the curtain. When they went to grab it, the thing flew out the window and right into their truck. Knocked itself right out. Did you want me to call them back to bring it?"

"No, I'm good," said Vegas as Eleanor made a face of disgust behind her.

"Sounds like they had an interesting evening," Eleanor said.

"They're always getting into the weirdest predicaments. Skunk got his foot stuck in a sewer drain several months ago. They had to call the fire department to get him out. It took about three jars of Vaseline, but they did it."

"Why would a fire department have three jars of Vaseline?" asked Eleanor.

"It was left over from their St. Patrick's Day celebration," Lazy said.

At that moment, they saw Skunk and Squirrel's truck pull into the parking lot. They parked beside Vegas' Volkswagen, then got out and waited for a woman to come out of the truck. She was just under five feet tall, wearing a Russian fur hat and what looked to Vegas like a long smock with flower patterns all over it.

Squirrel did the introductions. "Everybody, this is Gypsy Moth."

"Gypsy Moth?" Vegas asked in a bit of disbelief.

Squirrel added, "She is a descendent of Sitting Bull's sister, Standing Cow."

"Standing Cow?" Vegas said in the same tone.

Eleanor whispered to her daughter, "We are really adding to our interesting people list now!"

As Vegas and Eleanor and Pepsi got out of the Volkswagen, Gypsy Moth got down on her knees and laid her face against the parking lot pavement and began chanting. Vegas thought it sounded like "see coat tie," but she wasn't positive.

"What is she doing?" Vegas asked Squirrel in a whisper so as not to interfere with Gypsy Moth's whatever it was she was doing.

Squirrel answered, "She's getting into her meditative state so she can help us with the next clue."

Vegas watched as Gypsy Moth raised and lowered her face to the ground, using her right hand to hold her hat on her head.

"Are you sure that's what she's doing?" asked Vegas.

"Oh, yeah, she's a psychic, a gypsy, and a universal traveler," Squirrel said.

"Universal traveler?"

"She was abducted by aliens," Skunk said.

"I see they brought her back," Vegas said and watched Gypsy Moth complete her ritual. After she did, she stood up and walked to Vegas. She stared intently at her without speaking, making Vegas uncomfortable.

"Uh, I'm Vegas Chantly. This is my mother, Eleanor, and her cat Pepsi. But you probably already knew that."

Eleanor set Pepsi down and reached her hand out excitedly. "I'm very thrilled to meet you. I hope I don't give off any bad vibes. If I do, it's probably from that burger I ate earlier. It was good, though."

Gypsy Moth closed her eyes and let out a scream that

sounded like a duck caught in a boat propeller. Everybody was startled. Gypsy Moth then opened her eyes and stood nose to nose with Vegas. "I'm getting a reading on you."

"I'm starting to get one on you, too," said Vegas.

"Does Colorado mean anything to you?"

"It's a state."

Gypsy Moth closed her eyes for a few seconds, then opened them wide like she had just sat on a tack. "Your fate will be found in Colorado near the mighty aspens where only the deer and elk roam. Go there and you will become the finder of love."

"Let's go now!" said an excited Eleanor.

"I'm supposed to marry an elk?" Vegas asked.

Gypsy Moth replied, "No. Wait, I'm losing it. The reading is gone. I'm sorry. What are we doing next?"

Squirrel stepped forward. "We need you to help us solve the *Riddles and Riches* puzzle. I brought my puzzle to help you get some good vibes on it. Get the puzzle, Skunk."

"Will do," Skunk said and ran to the truck and got the puzzle box.

Squirrel took the box then dropped down to one knee in reverence to the one and only Gypsy Moth, and lifted it up to her. "I give you this puzzle in hopes that your supreme knowledge will show us the next clue and we can all get rich. Of course, we would only use the money for good and to buy the *Dukes of Hazzard* pinball machine at Ollie's house."

Gypsy Moth placed her hands on the puzzle box and breathed in deeply while closing her eyes and tilting her head back. "I am getting something ... something that will bring wealth to those that are gathered here tonight."

Skunk said with a big grin, "That's what we want to hear."

Gypsy Moth informed them, "We have to form a spirit circle."

"You mean like a rodeo?" asked Skunk.

Squirrel stood up and stared at Skunk disapprovingly. "No, it's not like at a rodeo. We're not going to start riding bulls here. Miss Gypsy Moth wants to read from the higher plane of spiritual consciousness. Right, Miss Gypsy Moth?"

"You speak the truth, long tail one," Gypsy Moth said. "We will need to form a spirit circle around a fire."

"Well, you can't have a fire in the parking lot," Lazy said. "We tried that once for the homecoming game and the pavement melted."

Gypsy Moth looked at Lazy. "Well, we've got to have a fire to reach the spiritual plane in the spirit circle. That's what the book says we have to do."

"No fire," said Lazy.

"Hey, I didn't write the book," said Gypsy Moth.

"No fire. I ain't telling you all again."

They all stared at each other, wondering what to do. Then Squirrel came up with an idea. "How about we use a flashlight instead?"

"A flashlight?" asked Gypsy Moth. "I've never done a spirit circle around a flashlight. I did one around a goat once, but it was blessed by a witch first."

"I don't know of any witches around here," said Squirrel. "But I could look one up on the internet. Do I need to tell her to bring a goat?"

"She would have to bless the puzzle," said Skunk.

"My sister is a witch," Lazy said. "Well, not a real witch. You know, just a jerk."

"She has to be a real witch or it doesn't count," stated Gypsy Moth.

Vegas suggested, "Since we don't have a goat and we're only using a flashlight for the spirit circle, maybe we could just use an electrician or a fireman to bless it."

"I'm a volunteer fireman," Skunk said. "I can bless the snot out of that puzzle."

They all looked at Gypsy Moth for verification. She said, "Sure, why not."

"I'll go get the flashlight," said an excited Skunk as he took off running toward the truck. "Don't start without me."

"We can't start without you, Skunk," shouted Squirrel. "You have to get the flashlight and bless it." He turned back to the group shaking his head in disbelief. "I don't think his ladder goes all the way up. Shoot, I don't even think he can find his ladder." Then Squirrel remembered something. "Ah, man, I forgot to bring the gong. I'm sorry, Vegas."

"It's okay."

"But it's part of the ceremony to make you an observer."

"We'll just high-five," said Vegas, and they did.

A few moments later Skunk came running holding the flashlight above his head for all to see. "I have the flame of knowledge!"

Gypsy Moth walked away from the group and walked around the parking lot until she found a spot she liked. "Place the flame of knowledge here."

Skunk rushed to the spot and placed the flashlight on the pavement and stepped back. Gypsy

Moth said to Skunk, "You have to turn it on."

"Sorry. This is my first spirit circle."

Skunk turned the flashlight on, and its strong light shone right in Gypsy Moth's eyes, which caused her to step to one side.

"Okay, how do I bless the flame of knowledge?" asked Skunk.

Gypsy Moth went through the instructions. "You stand over it and throw this gypsy powder on it."

Gypsy Moth reached into her pocket and pulled out a handful of powder, then placed it into Skunk's hand.

"What exactly is that powder?" asked Vegas.

"Flour that's been blessed by one of the elders," said Gypsy Moth.

"Which elder?" asked Squirrel.

"It was blessed by Tyler down at the hospital."

"Is he a doctor?" asked Eleanor.

"He's the night janitor," Gypsy Moth said.

"A janitor can bless flour and that gives it special powers?" Vegas asked in disbelief.

Gypsy Moth responded, "It doesn't get its special power from being flour. It gets its special power from being in my right-hand pocket."

Skunk took the special flour powder and threw it on the flame of knowledge.

Gypsy Moth told Skunk, "Now repeat after me. I come forward in peace."

"I come forward in peace."

"To find the great spirits of the sky."

"To find the great spirits of the sky."

"That I as a policeman."

"Fireman. I'm a volunteer fireman."

"I thought you were a policeman," said Gypsy Moth.

"Fireman."

"Whatever," Gypsy Moth sighed. "That I as a volunteer fireman."

"That I as a volunteer fireman."

"Do bless this light to bring our spirits together."

"Do bless this light to bring our spirits together."

"Okay, the sucker's blessed," said Gypsy Moth.

"What are we going to do now?" asked Squirrel.

"Séance," said Gypsy Moth.

"Ance," Eleanor said.

Vegas rolled her eyes and shook her head. "No, Mom, you don't say ance, it's a séance."

Eleanor looked at her daughter as if she was trying to figure out an abstract painting. Then it hit her. "So you say it to yourself."

"Whatever, Mom."

Gypsy Moth then gave instructions to the group. "We all now form a circle around the flame of knowledge and hold hands."

Squirrel moved to Vegas's side so he could hold her hand. Vegas frowned but took his hand.

Gypsy Moth closed her eyes and began. "I, the one and only Gypsy Moth, call upon my avatar Standing Cow to come forth and give me knowledge of this game called *Riddles and Riches*. We seek help in finding what the next clue is. Give us a sign of your presence. Just one little sign."

Eleanor sneezed.

"I'm sorry," Eleanor said. "Wait, was that the sign? Is Standing Cow in my mind?"

"Nothing is in your mind, Mom," whispered Vegas.

"No," Gypsy Moth said. "Your mother has the avatar Standing Cow visiting her. Don't hold back, dear lady. Let her use you as a vessel to bring forth her great knowledge."

"I am so excited right now," Eleanor said as she closed her eyes and attempted to focus. "I see something green. It's shaped like a bowl of Jell-O and it's talking."

"What's it saying?" asked Squirrel in a whisper.

"It's saying let them eat all the Jell-O."

Vegas rolled her eyes. "Mom, stop this."

"Don't interrupt a psychic when they're in a trance," stated Gypsy Moth. "It could knock their mind all out of whack."

"Her mind has been out of whack for some time."

Skunk said, "I bet it's that restaurant down at Kipsey. They have a Jell-O platter."

"That's amazing," said Squirrel. "How did you come up with that?"

"Sometimes the genius genie just hits me upside the head."

Squirrel replied, "The only thing that hits me upside the head is Mom."

Everyone looked up as a police car pulled into the parking lot with its lights flashing. An officer in a blue uniform standing less than five feet tall got out of the car and walked to the group.

"I'm Officer Brandon Hollister the third."

"There are three of you?" asked Vegas.

"I'm the tall one. We got a report that something crazy was going on down at the Lazy Susan parking lot."

"You'd be right," Vegas said under her breath.

"Are you all a cult or something?" Officer Hollister asked.

"No," replied Gypsy Moth. "We're a group of people seeking knowledge."

"You all aren't sacrificing anything down here, are you?"

"Just our dignity," replied Vegas.

Eleanor began looking about in a panic. "Where's Pepsi?"

"What?" asked Vegas.

"I lost Pepsi. You don't think I was concentrating on my reading so much that I popped him into a vortex of lost time, do you?"

"I'm pretty sure that didn't happen, Mom."

Officer Hollister said, "Ma'am, there's a soda machine over there if you're thirsty."

"Pepsi is her cat," Vegas said.

"She believes a soda is a cat?" asked the officer.

"No," Vegas replied and tried to clarify. "Pepsi is an actual cat. She found him in a soda machine, so she called him Pepsi."

Officer Hollister looked at Vegas quizzically. "I'm not following."

Vegas groaned in frustration. She felt like she was going to blow up like a volcano in an eighth-grade science class. "I'm not surprised. The whole evening has been like this. I'm surrounded by a bunch of nuts. I got one that thinks she's some sort of psychic called Gypsy Moth, then there are two guys named Skunk and Squirrel, the woman that runs the motel here is called Lazy, and my mother is, well, my mother, and now here comes little boy blue. This is too much crazy for one woman to deal with on a warm Georgia night!"

No one knew what to say. Vegas puffed up her cheeks like a chipmunk with a mouthful of nuts and slowly blew the air out of her mouth. "I'm sorry," Vegas said before she added, "Though I'm positive that a court of law would find in my favor."

They all just stared at Vegas.

Vegas looked about, trying not to look at their faces in the glow of the flame of knowledge. "I'll go look for the cat," she said.

As Vegas walked toward the motel, she could hear her mother talking to the officer. "I'm getting a reading on you. Is your favorite color red? Wait, no, that's me."

Vegas went to the soda machine thinking that Pepsi had gone back home after all the craziness he had just gone through. She looked around and even placed her ear against the soda machine to see if she could hear him inside, but she didn't see or hear any sign of him. She then walked around the side of the motel. A narrow path meandered around the motel, with a steep hill beside it that led down to a wooded ravine.

At the back of the motel, Vegas saw an outdoor light nailed to a tree. A thick black wire ran from it to the motel meter box; it obviously had not been done by a professional electrician.

She looked at the illuminated tree base and saw Pepsi sniffing at an orange salamander while flicking his tail back and forth.

Vegas walked to Pepsi and picked him up. "There you are. Listen, running away from my mother isn't going to work. I've already tried that. A lot. She has some kind of invisible web attached to us so we can't get away."

Vegas saw an old grill leaned against the tree with its lid askew and its right wheel missing. Just above the barbecue lid was an old metal sign with peeling paint nailed to the tree. She brushed aside some vines that were growing over it. It read, "Go Atlanta Falcons."

"The Falcon Tree," she said to herself. Vegas looked down at Pepsi in her arms. "This is the second time you've led me to a clue. You are definitely a better investigator than Mom. In fact, you may be a better investigator than me."

Vegas looked around the tree and noticed the ground beneath the barbecue was covered in gravel. She kicked around the ground and realized how hard it would be to dig there, especially with the broken shovel she had.

She walked around the tree and saw that there was about two feet of flat ground covered in grass before the earth dropped down to a steep embankment that went down into the ravine.

"I'm going to have to get something better to dig with. And we better get you back to the group before they cast a spell or something," Vegas said.

When Vegas got back, everyone was gone except for Eleanor.

"You found him!" Eleanor said with a smile as she reached out for Pepsi. She hugged him tightly against her chest. "Mommy missed you. Where was he?"

"He was playing with a salamander in the back. Where did everybody go?"

"Officer Hollister told us that we all had to disburse because we were freaking out all the passersby. What do we do now?"

"We're going to Walmart."

"Walmart? Oh, I always enjoy shopping after a night out on the town. It helps me come down from all the excitement."

"What excitement?"

"You know, meeting people and doing readings."

"You can't do readings, Mom."

"I was doing pretty well tonight. I think it's my calling."

"You can't do readings, Mom, because there's no such thing."

"Gypsy Moth disagrees with you."

Vegas just shook her head. "Let's just go hang out with the crazy people at Walmart for a while now. Okay?"

CHAPTER 23

AS THEY PULLED into the parking lot, Eleanor said, "The twenty-four-hour Walmart is the greatest invention ever."

"Yeah, it ranks right up there with sliced bread and penicillin."

Vegas got out of the vehicle and waited for her mother to crawl out. As she helped her mother up, two people walked by staring at them in befuddlement. Eleanor had Pepsi in her arms and her large purse slung over her shoulder like a diaper bag.

"You can't take Pepsi inside the Walmart. They don't want him climbing all over their ceiling either."

"They probably allow service animals."

Vegas shook her head. "He's not a service animal."

"I can't just leave him in the vehicle. He might think I abandoned him."

"He won't think that – he's trying to get away from you like I've been doing for the past twenty years. Now, put him in the vehicle and we'll be right back."

Eleanor frowned. "But what if he gets too hot?"

"I got an idea. Why don't you stay out here with him? I'll only be in there for a few minutes."

"But I want to go," Eleanor said with a pouty mouth.

"So you're going in with me?"

"I don't want to leave him."

"So you're staying out here with him?"

Eleanor was quiet for a few seconds. "I don't know what to do. Can you help me?"

"You've been beyond help for a long time now. Listen, I'm going in. You decide what you're going to do."

Vegas walked away and before she got to the entrance, Eleanor called out. "Wait up! I'm coming with you!"

Vegas waited for her mother to catch up. "So you decided to leave Pepsi in the vehicle?" she asked.

"Yes. He probably needs some alone time to work out his goals for the future."

"Uh-huh," Vegas said. As they walked in the store, Vegas heard meowing. She stopped and stared at her mother. "What was that?"

"Oh, it was my stomach growling," Eleanor said guiltily. "I really should get something to eat."

"You brought that cat in here, didn't you?" whispered Vegas.

"He's hidden on me," whispered Eleanor.

"Hidden on you?" Vegas whispered incredulously.

"He's in my purse."

"He better be. Now come on, and tell Pepsi to be quiet. We don't want to get into trouble with a Walmart cop."

Eleanor whispered into her purse. "You be quiet in there, Pepsi. We don't want people staring at us."

Several people walked by staring at them. Vegas sighed and went to find the garden center.

"What exactly are we looking for?" asked Eleanor.

"Digging tools. My shovel is broken."

"This is a strange time to take up gardening."

"I'm not."

Eleanor abruptly stopped at a group of round tables that were on sale. "Look at these tables," she said. Vegas reluctantly stopped and walked back to her mother.

"I need you to stay focused here. I'm always telling you that, by the way."

"I remember back when I was in high school we were at a Christmas party and me and my buddies Frieda, Tammy, and Pat got up on some tables like these and started dancing. Boy, the eggnog was flowing that night," Eleanor said with a hearty laugh. "We were a bunch of nuts, but we had fun."

"While I'm slightly disturbed at the thought of you dancing on a table, I'm glad you had fun with your buddies. Now, let's go get some digging tools."

"Right, chief," Eleanor said with a salute.

They made their way to the shovels and Vegas looked them over. Eleanor reached into her pocket and pulled out her Chapstick, which she promptly dropped onto the floor. She got on her knees and began searching for it. Just then, Vegas noticed her mother on all fours with her butt stuck in the air.

"What are you doing?" whispered Vegas in a voice of shock.

"I dropped my Chapstick and it rolled under this shelf. I see it, but I can't quite reach it. Can you get it?"

Vegas' blood pressure rose. "Every time I go with you anywhere, some sort of bizarre puppet show pops up."

Vegas got on her knees to retrieve the Chapstick but couldn't reach it. She stood up, grabbed one of the shovels, got back down, and used the shovel handle to maneuver the Chapstick out from under the shelf. As it rolled toward another shelf, Vegas grabbed it and then handed it to her mother.

"Here, now put it in your pocket and don't get it back out."

"That was pretty fancy how you used that shovel."

"I'm always learning new ways to rescue you, it seems like."

Eleanor slipped the Chapstick back into her pocket and watched her daughter put the shovel back on the rack and grab a pick ax.

"I think this will work," said Vegas. "I'll get both a shovel and a pick ax."

"I wouldn't mind going back and getting that table we looked at earlier."

"We don't have time to buy you a dancing table."

"But it would look great in my living room under the mirror."

"We have no way to get it home to your mirror. Let's go."

At checkout, Vegas started to put the items on the counter when Eleanor grabbed her daughter by the arm and whispered, "Look at what we're buying."

"A shovel and an ax," Vegas whispered back.

"I know. People are going to think we're burying a body."

"Mom," Vegas whispered in frustration.

"I'll get a Hershey bar so it doesn't look suspicious."

"Mom, that's not – fine, make it two."

"Gotcha," Eleanor said and placed another candy bar on the conveyor belt.

"Hello," said the clerk.

"Hello," said Eleanor. "How are you?"

"I'm fine."

Vegas noticed Eleanor staring at the clerk and was about to intervene when her mother said, "I think I'm getting a reading on you."

Vegas grabbed her mother's arm. "Mom, don't."

"A what?" asked the clerk.

"I just discovered that I have clairvoyance."

"It's more like clair-annoyance," said Vegas.

Eleanor ignored her daughter and went on trying to use her new skill. "Do you like to dance?"

The clerk was startled. "You mean now?"

"I mean ever."

"Uh, no."

Eleanor seemed hurt by her response. "Are you sure?"

"Yes."

"I think she knows if she likes to dance," Vegas said. "Now leave the nice lady alone."

Eleanor would not be deterred. "Maybe you dance in your sleep and you don't know it, and that's what I'm reading."

"Mom, you're not a psychic."

"Yes, I am."

"Are you going to start riding around on a broom now?" asked Vegas.

"That's not what a psychic is and you know it," Eleanor said angrily.

The clerk looked at the two of them as if she wished they were somewhere else.

Eleanor then noticed a man in line in the next aisle behind the clerk. "Hmm, maybe I'm reading the man behind you. Would you tap him on the shoulder and ask him if he likes to dance?"

At that moment, Pepsi popped his head out of Eleanor's purse and began meowing. A look of panic crossed Eleanor's face before she said shakily, "It's okay. He's a service animal."

"Service animal?" asked the clerk. She turned to Vegas and asked, "Does she have a handicap of some kind?"

"Yeah, she's crazy," Vegas said.

They paid and Vegas retrieved the shovel, pick ax, and candy bars. She headed toward the exit but didn't realize her mother wasn't following. She was smiling at the clerk and telling her, "You should take up dancing. I can see in the future, so you can trust me." Then she promptly ran into a display and knocked a bunch of snacks off the shelf, spilling them all over the floor.

"I'm so sorry," Eleanor said and began picking them up.

"It's okay," said the clerk. "I'll pick this all up."

"No. I clean up my own messes. Which is probably why I'm tired all the time."

"It's fine," the clerk insisted as she squatted down. "This is why they pay me minimum wage."

Vegas came back to see what was taking her mother so long when she saw them both squatting down to pick up snacks.

"Are you two fighting?" asked Vegas.

"No," said Eleanor. "Me and – what was your name, sweetie?"

"Traci."

A look of astonishment crossed Eleanor's face. "I was going to say Traci! Well, right after Bertha. My psychic powers are real."

"Mom, she has a nametag on that says her name. Now, what are you two doing on the floor?"

"I just knocked this display over. You know, I don't think I've ever gone into a store and not knocked something over. I guess it's because my mind is always working."

"That hasn't happened for some time," Vegas said as she helped her mother up and led her outside, to the great relief of Traci.

"I still think she was a dancer," said Eleanor. "Of course, I just discovered my calling, so I'll have to practice some with it first."

"You're not a psychic. You're just a mom trying to find her place in the world and you don't know what the password is,"

Vegas said as she put the pick ax and shovel in the backseat with the handles jutting into the front.

"How am I going to crawl over the handles?" Eleanor asked, and began to try.

"Use your genie skills."

"You mean psychic skills, baby."

"Whatever. Just hurry up."

"Oh!" she said. "I think me and your shovel are dating now."

"Well, he's going to regret that," Vegas said as she stared out across the top of her Volkswagen and saw a giant Paul Bunyan statue in the distance. Somehow it was appropriate, a strange landscape feature to punctuate her strange shopping experience.

Eleanor finally got situated, and Vegas got in, and she and her psychic mother headed back to the Lazy Susan.

CHAPTER 24

VEGAS PULLED the Volkswagen to the side of the road near the woods just before they got to the Lazy Susan Motel.

"What's wrong?" Eleanor asked. "Do you have to go to the bathroom? You should have gone back at Walmart. Do you need me to help you?"

"I don't have to go to the bathroom, nor do I need any help from you if I did. I just don't want anybody to know what we're doing."

Eleanor stared at her daughter intently for a few seconds before asking, "What are we doing?"

Vegas closed her eyes in search of some inner peace before opening them again to see her mother staring at her and Pepsi clinging to the ceiling. "Mom, we're digging for clues that lead to a treasure on somebody else's property. This could cause all kinds of problems."

"Do you think we could be shot or something?" Eleanor asked as she plucked her cat off the ceiling and put him in her lap.

"Anything's possible when it comes to treasure. Now, I need you to be as quiet as possible. I know that's against your nature, but you have to do it."

"I can do it," Eleanor said with a whisper. "Let me get my purse."

"Why do you need your purse?"

"To put my baby in," Eleanor said as she picked up the purse from the floorboard and placed Pepsi inside. He sat in it proudly, his head sticking out, ready for a grand adventure. "I can't leave Pepsi in here. He can help us find the treasure."

"Whatever. Now, we have to be quiet and do this as quickly and efficiently as possible so nobody finds out we're here. Got it?"

"My lips are locked and I swallowed the key," Eleanor said as she went through the motions of locking her lips and swallowing the key.

"Mom, you can't lock your lips, then swallow the key."

"That's right. But if I swallow the key first, how am I going to lock my lips? We are in a quandary here."

"Mom, just be as quiet as possible."

"I can throw it over my shoulder," Eleanor said and mimed the motions. She then started giggling and put her hand over her mouth.

"You're going to need a bigger lock," whispered Vegas as she tried to keep from smiling at her giggling mother.

Vegas got out of the car, and before she could tell her mother to wait, she was crawling over the tools and got stuck on them.

"Let me get the tools out first," whispered Vegas.

"My heel is stuck under the dashboard somehow. Something grabbed me! Wait, it was just the gearshift."

Vegas tried maneuvering the tools out of the way so her mother could get across, but it wasn't working. She suggested gently, "You have to move back to your seat or you'll impale yourself."

"I can't move because my foot is stuck."

"You have to move or I can't get the tools out."

"You need to get the passenger door fixed."

"I wouldn't have to do that if you didn't try to break into it to start with."

"So this is my fault?"

"All of my problems are your fault," Vegas said.

Vegas pushed her mother back into her seat with some effort, then stood up and caught her breath.

"I'll see if I can get the tools out first," she said after a moment. "You don't move."

"I don't see how this is going to work," said Eleanor.

"I got them in here, I can get them out."

"This is kind of like that Rubik's Cube thing isn't it? There's only one way to get everything to line up, and let's be honest here, we got no idea what that is."

Vegas tried to get the tools out, but it seemed like the seats and dashboard were in the way no matter what angle the tools were placed at. After what seemed like hours, she finally got the pick ax and shovel out of the car, and her mother and Pepsi soon followed.

"That was like being baptized in a salt shaker," said Eleanor.

"Come on," Vegas said, and started walking toward the motel.

They quietly made their way toward the back and stood at the tree with the Atlanta Falcons sign on it.

Eleanor asked, "Why exactly are we at this spot?"

Vegas set her tools down and pulled out her notebook and opened it up. "The last clue was *Lazy Susan can provide you rest. At the Falcon Tree it knows best. In the bottle a clue does nest. It will take you to riches blessed.* The tree has grown all around the Falcons sign, so it's been here for some time now."

"The clue didn't say anything about a sign growing into a tree," Eleanor said.

"That doesn't matter, it's the Falcon Tree."

"I think it's a maple, but to be honest, I'm not really good at identifying trees. The only tree that I can identify for sure is a Christmas tree. Maybe we can figure out what kind of tree it is if we rub it." Eleanor rubbed the tree. "What is a maple tree supposed to feel like, anyway?"

"It doesn't matter what kind of tree it is. The sign makes it a Falcon tree, which is the clue, and the sign– Oh, never mind," Vegas said in frustration.

She put down her notebook and started digging at the base of the tree with the pick ax. After some hard digging for ten minutes, she found a bottle. It was an old RC Cola bottle that was sealed on top with duct tape.

"You found it!" Eleanor said. "You know, I lost my radio that I had in the closet of the guest room. I know it was there last year because it fell off and hit me on top of the head. That smarted. And you know what? The radio came on. It was an ad for back cream. The announcer said, 'Do you have a sore back? Then you need–' Well, I can't remember the name of the cream. I wonder if it would have worked on my head."

Vegas put her hand over her mother's mouth. "Why are you telling me this?" she whispered.

"I thought you could help me find the radio. I've been very impressed with your finding skills these past couple of days."

"How do you lose a radio?"

"Well, obviously you put it in my house."

Vegas turned her attention back to the bottle. She worked the tape off the bottle. Inside was a piece of paper. She turned the bottle upside down and shook it until the paper slid out enough so she could pull it out the rest of the way. She unrolled it and walked into the light that was nailed to the tree.

"Where's the treasure?" asked Eleanor excitedly.

"It says, 'You found clue four, now venture to the giant, and you will find the door.'"

They looked at each other. "Giant?" asked Eleanor. "What giant?"

It hit Vegas almost immediately. "Paul Bunyan."

"He's a giant all right, but I don't think he's real."

"No. Back at Walmart when you were trying to get into the vehicle, I saw a giant statue of Paul Bunyan."

Eleanor looked at her daughter curiously. "Are you having a spell?"

"No. I saw it. That's the next place we have to go."

"Well, can't we do that tomorrow? I'm getting mighty tired."

"What time is it anyway?"

Eleanor looked at her watch. "It's one in the morning."

"Oh, it's later than I thought. But we have to keep going. Hand me your phone."

"We're at a motel," Eleanor said and searched her purse for her phone before finally finding it and handing it to Vegas. "Why can't we just get a room here for the night?"

"Because I don't want them to know we're here," Vegas said as she began snapping pictures of the clue.

"Why not?"

"They'll find our clue. The Snodgrass brothers would get a jump on everybody else trying to solve the puzzle."

"The Snodgrass brothers are strange children, aren't they?"

"Yes, they are," Vegas said. She finished photographing the clues and put them back into the hole next to the tree, then recorded the coordinates.

As they began to walk back to the Volkswagen, they turned to see a woman standing with her arms crossed in the outdoor light with a menacing look on her face.

Eleanor looked at Vegas and said, "Uh-oh. There's going to be a rumble."

CHAPTER 25

VEGAS, Eleanor and Pepsi looked at the woman bathed in the overhead tree light. She was short and very thin. She had shoulder-length gray hair with a pair of black eyeglasses perched on the end of her slender nose.

"Did you find it?" she asked.

Vegas tried to think of a good answer but failed to do so. "Find what?"

"The clue," the woman said as she shook her head in disgust.

Vegas and Eleanor looked at each other, confused about how she knew about the clue. Eleanor decided to take the lead. "We're just here walking our cat."

"If you're walking your cat, then why is it in your purse?"

Eleanor glanced at her daughter, then back at the woman. "What purse?"

"You two are obviously related to one another," the woman said in a monotone voice.

"Who are you?" asked Vegas.

"I'm Susan Snodgrass. I'm the Susan of the Lazy Susan Motel here."

"So you're kin to the Snodgrass brothers?" asked Vegas.

"They're my nephews," replied Susan.

"My condolences," Eleanor said.

"Thank you, though I'm not sure you actually mean it."

"Oh, we've been around them," Vegas said. "We mean it."

"You know, I've never seen them work a day in their lives. I don't know how they bought that new truck of theirs."

"I guess some people just have that skill," Vegas said.

"I'd rather not talk about my nephews right now. It kind of makes me nauseous. Now, did you find the clue?" Susan asked.

"What makes you think we were looking for a clue?" asked Vegas.

"My daughter told me what you were all doing down here tonight," Susan informed them.

"The séance didn't make any sense to me, but then she told me that Gypsy Moth was going to help you all to look for clues for the puzzle, so I thought you might have found it. I knew my nephews wouldn't find the clues because they might just be the stupidest two people on God's earth."

"Did you know a clue to the puzzle was here all this time?" asked Vegas.

"Yeah, I helped Walter bury it."

"Walter?" Eleanor asked. "Who's Walter?"

"The guy who created the puzzle, Mom, Walter Peabody," Vegas said. "You knew him?"

"Yeah, see, my husband left me a few months before I met Walter. It was my fault that my husband left me."

"You shouldn't blame yourself," Eleanor said in a concerned voice.

"No, it was my fault. I locked all the doors and wouldn't let him back into the house. So I kind of moped about for a while, then I met Walter at a chainsaw wood-carving class. We kind of hit it off. He was a great dancer, too. We got close, and he told me what he was doing with the puzzle and all."

"Did he tell you anything about his boss, Davis Harper?" asked Vegas.

"He said he didn't trust him. He was a big-time gambler, and Walter did not take to gambling. He thought it was the work of the devil. But he loved treasure hunting. I told him that some people look at treasure hunting as gambling, too. He said sometimes it is if you aren't sure there's a treasure to begin with, and so he wanted to create a real one. So that's what got him interested in it. He was always a big-time collector of things. Not just junk things – he had a lot of valuable things. The treasure is real and is worth a lot of money."

"You saw the treasure?" Vegas asked.

"I did. I looked inside, and it was filled with all kinds of items. He sealed it up in a weatherproof container so none of the fragile objects like the baseball cards and comic books would get wet. He had gold and silver coins in there, too. It wasn't just pop culture valuables, either. Then he put it in a box that almost looked like a coffin, then he took it out somewhere and buried it."

Vegas thought Susan was telling the truth. "Tell me more about his relationship with Mr. Harper."

"Not a whole lot more to tell, really. Mr. Harper did a hostile takeover of the company to begin with, and pretty much robbed it for his gambling obsession. I wasn't surprised when I learned he was selling the company. He probably needs to in order to pay down his debts. Walter didn't trust giving him the information about the clues because he was afraid he would steal it for his gambling obsession. So he paid him ten thousand dollars to leave him alone while he worked on it."

Vegas said, "It all makes sense. ... Say, why didn't you ever tell anybody about the clue here on your property? Or any of the others?"

"I promised Walter I wouldn't."

"Most people would either be dying to tell someone or just take it for themselves."

"I guess it was kind of neat to me that nobody knew about this clue except me. And, well, now you two. Like I said, I was starting to fall in love with Walter. I would never betray him, but he left to go live in the woods. He wanted to be by himself and get away from the rat race. So we parted ways. I always wondered where he went to. It was exciting for me to help him hide this and to know it was on my property. We buried it here on a summer night when nobody was at the motel. It was kind of romantic, too."

"Did you help him bury the other clues?" asked Vegas.

"No, just this one."

"Have you ever seen anybody come here looking for it?" asked Vegas.

"To my knowledge, not a single person has ever gotten this far. You must be pretty good at it. Congratulations."

"She gets her detective skills from me," bragged Eleanor.

"Are you Eleanor?" asked Susan.

"Yes. How did you know that? Oh, my goodness, did you do a reading on me? Or did I read myself and project it out? This is a new superpower for me, so I haven't gotten it fully under control yet."

"No. You just fit the description my daughter gave about you."

Eleanor was disappointed. "Oh. Well, I guess I do stand out."

"You definitely do that," Vegas mumbled.

"Did the note in the bottle help you figure out the next clue?" asked Susan.

"Yeah, I guess you already know what it is."

"No. Walter never let me know what this one said. All I did

was help him bury it. I wish you all the best of luck in your treasure hunt. I'll be seeing you around."

"That's it?" asked a confused Vegas. "Aren't you curious about where the treasure is?"

"Walter was my treasure," Susan said. She then turned and left, and Vegas and Eleanor watched her disappear around the corner of the motel.

"Now what do we do?" asked Eleanor.

"We got a date with a giant man."

Eleanor's phone rang, sounding as loud as a siren at this time of night. She frantically dug inside her purse for her phone and retrieved it. She looked at the number and said, "It's Sergeant Miller."

Vegas took the phone. "Hello?"

"Do you know how hard it is to get a hold of you?" asked a grumpy Sergeant Miller.

"I have an active life. It's kind of late for you to be calling."

"I'm working late at the office tonight so I thought I'd give you another try. I also was hoping to wake you up like you did me."

"I can understand that. What do you want?"

"I ran the license plate on that truck for you."

"Oh, I guess we don't need it now. We know the owners are Snodgrass."

"Snodgrass?" he said in a confused voice.

"They call themselves Squirrel and Skunk, but I'm guessing it's registered under their real names."

"Squirrel and Skunk?" asked Sergeant Miller.

"It's a long story," said Vegas.

"The truck isn't registered to Snodgrass or any animals."

"Who is it registered to?" asked Vegas.

"Davis Harper."

Vegas stood holding the phone confused.

CHAPTER 26

VEGAS DROVE them to the Paul Bunyan statue she had seen earlier as she reasoned over the new evidence that Sergeant Miller had given her.

"How did the Snodgrass brothers meet up with Mr. Harper?" Vegas asked herself aloud.

"Maybe they're kin somehow," Eleanor said. "I'm sure we have a lot of creepy cousins and the like roaming around our family."

"And they always followed us like they knew where we were going. How is that possible?"

"Yellow does stand out in a crowd. That's why they used canaries in the coal mines as warnings. They were easier to see."

"That's not how that worked."

Eleanor frowned. "How did it work then?"

"If the canary died, then the miners knew the air was bad and they had to get out."

A look of horror crossed Eleanor's face. "That's terrible!"

Vegas focused on her own conundrum. "Wait a minute. The first time we saw the Snodgrass brothers' truck was at the Dixie Discount."

Eleanor tried to remember the Dixie Discount excursion as she began nodding her head in agreement. "Yeah ... I remember that. I bought a lamp. What did you buy?"

"I bought the *Riddle and Riches* puzzle. That's why we're here."

Eleanor pointed at her head with her index finger as if to show she had a great memory. "I knew you bought something."

Vegas continued. "Then they kept following us."

"I guess that's what they were hired to do by that publisher guy. What was his name?"

"His name is Davis Harper, mom. But why did he want us followed, being that he was the one who hired us to start with?"

"I guess he wanted to keep track of us."

"Maybe he thought I might steal the treasure for myself," Vegas thought.

"Or, now hear me out – he's in love with you," Eleanor said.

"He's not in love with me."

"Oh, my word, he's in love with *me*," Eleanor said with surprise. "He is handsome. Could you imagine me with a younger man? Oh, the things I could teach him."

Vegas ignored her mother and thought about all the possible scenarios. She remembered that she got in the truck at the Horses and Problems ranch to move it out of the way. That could be the key. She had to check out her hunch. She pulled into the Walmart parking lot and drove to a parking space beneath a parking lot light pole. She got out.

"What are you doing?" asked Eleanor. "I thought we were going to see the big man."

Vegas walked to the rear of the vehicle and placed her hand into the wheel well and began feeling around.

Eleanor stuck her head out of the driver's side door while lying across the seat. "What are you doing?"

Vegas kept feeling around the wheel well and felt something. She pulled it out and saw an antenna device. She took it to her mother.

"Do you see this?" asked Vegas.

"Yeah, but don't take it off, the tire might fall off or something. Put it back on."

"It's not to keep the tire on, Mom, it's a tracking device. I bet they put this here at the Dixie Discount."

"How did you know they did that?"

"They kept appearing where we were. There was no other answer. They're too stupid to find us on their own. And when I got into their truck, I saw some sort of monitor on the dashboard that I didn't understand at the time. Now I know that's what they were using to track us."

"But how did you know it was under the tire well and not some other place on the vehicle?"

"When we got the flat and they fixed it, they seemed determined that they fix it and not us."

"I bet they took their shirts off to distract us so we wouldn't notice them fiddling with the device."

"I guess they did. I do wish they had just fired a gun into the air to distract us instead – that was a lot of ugly."

"What are you going to do with the devicey thing?" asked Eleanor.

Vegas looked around and saw a trash can. She took the tracking device and threw it inside and walked back to the vehicle, got inside and drove toward the Paul Bunyan statue.

"Maybe we should just drop this case," suggested Eleanor.

"Nope, I'm seeing it through. I'm guessing that Mr. Harper has already stolen the treasure and gambled it away, so my finding an empty box means he can't sell his company. It all makes sense now. Well, one of the ways it could make sense. I wasn't supposed to be able to find the treasure. He probably hired me just to make it look like he was trying to find it so he could sell the company. He then hired the Snodgrass brothers to keep tabs on me so they could report back what was happening and interfere to slow me down."

"That little scoundrel," said Eleanor. "I'm not dating him now."

The yellow Volkswagen pulled up to the twenty-foot high Paul Bunyan statue. They got out of the vehicle and stood staring up at Paul Bunyan, who was illuminated by lights at its base.

"Look at the size of that big man." exclaimed Eleanor. "This is the best vacation ever."

"It's not a vacation, Mom. There's a sign over here."

They walked to the sign and Vegas read it aloud. "This statue of Paul Bunyan was donated to the Georgia Park Service by the Flat Bottom, Georgia, Museum because they didn't have any idea what to do with it."

They looked at each other.

"That's touching," said Eleanor.

"It sounds like they just wanted to get rid of the thing."

"I wonder who built it."

Vegas examined the plaque. "It doesn't say."

"I wonder who gave it to the museum."

"I don't know."

"I wouldn't mind having it in my yard."

"Why on earth would you want a giant statue of Paul Bunyan in your yard?"

"I could sell tickets to come see the big man. I'd buy one."

"You'd buy a ticket to see your own statue?"

"It would be a sales device. People would see me walking in

with my ticket and they would want one, too. Your mommy is always thinking."

"Call it what you want," Vegas said as she looked at the statue of fiberglass and bright colors. "The clue said that we had to venture to the door at the foot of the giant."

Vegas walked to the back of Paul Bunyan and found a door at its right leg. Vegas tried opening it, but it was locked.

"I'll go get the shovel and see if I can get this door open. Hopefully it won't take me as long to get it out of the vehicle as the last time."

"I'll go get it. Where is it?"

Vegas narrowed her eyes at her mother. "It's in the vehicle."

"I remember now. Mommy and Pepsi will be right back. Come on Pepsi, we've got hero work to do." The cat meowed.

Eleanor walked off and Vegas tried the door again while slamming her shoulder into it. This time it opened.

Vegas rubbed her shoulder for a few seconds, then found a light switch and flipped it on. She looked around and saw wiring and a switchbox, which obviously ran the floodlights. She looked above her and saw a manila envelope in the rafters. She grabbed it and opened it.

Inside was a typed letter that was encased inside a Mylar sheet. It read, "Go to the place where the booger does roam. The swamp is sloppy and through it you must comb. Go to the Morris Tree above the moors. Then the treasure you seek will be yours."

"Vegas! It's stuck!" Eleanor yelled.

Vegas hurried to the vehicle, where she saw her mother desperately trying to get the shovel out of the Volkswagen.

"Mom, you don't have to get it out now. I found the clue."

"Thank goodness. I was beginning to think I would be wrestling that shovel until the end of time. What's the clue?"

"We have to go to Sloppy Swamp."

"Sloppy Swamp? Isn't that where Pepper and his buddy went to look for the Wood Booger?"

"Yeah. And we need to go to the Morris Tree."

"What's the Morris Tree?"

"I'm hoping Pepper will be able to tell us. Let's get us some pictures and establish the coordinates, then get out of here."

Eleanor took out her phone and took pictures of the area and the typed letter that was found in the manila envelope. After she finished, she looked at Vegas and asked, "Should we go on? I mean, it seems like the man that hired us is going to try and make sure we don't find what he hired us to find."

"I owe it to the company that's buying his. They want to know if the treasure still exists, and now so do I. Let's get back home and see if we can get a hold of Pepper."

"What if we can't reach him?"

"I'll go into Sloppy Swamp by myself."

"My baby isn't going into something called Sloppy Swamp alone. I'll go with you."

"Mom, it'll be too dangerous."

"My middle name is danger," Eleanor said proudly.

Vegas looked at her mother with her purse strap hung over her shoulder and Pepsi sticking out of it meowing.

"Danger isn't really the first word I think of when I look at you. Now, let's go."

CHAPTER 27

THE MORNING SUN began to rise over the mountains of Blue Falls, Georgia, as Vegas drove her Volkswagen into her mother's driveway. She shut off the engine and looked at her mother, who was asleep with her head against the window. Pepsi was asleep in her lap gently purring.

Vegas nudged her mother. "Mom, you're home. You can go inside and go to sleep."

Eleanor said groggily, "Where's the big man?"

"We left the big man in Flat Bottom."

Eleanor rubbed her eyes with her left hand and tried not to wake Pepsi. "Where are we?

"You're home."

"Our vacation is over?"

Vegas sighed. "Mom, for the last time, it wasn't a vacation, it was my case. There never was a vacation."

Eleanor yawned. "What time is it?"

"When I drove through town, the bank clock said it was 6:05. Let me help you get your things, then you can go inside, lie down, and get some rest."

Vegas got out of the vehicle and waited while Eleanor crawled over the shovel and ax and out the driver's side door.

Vegas helped her up and picked up Pepsi while she waited for her mother to find her keys in her large purse.

After a bit, Vegas said, "You do have them, don't you?"

"They're here somewhere."

"Hold Pepsi and I'll look for them."

Eleanor took Pepsi and Vegas began digging through her mother's purse.

"Why do you have such a large purse anyway?"

"So I can store my valuables. A girl needs a large purse to keep those things."

"I don't see any valuables in here," Vegas said as she pulled out a can. "There's a can of Beanie Weenies in here."

"That's what that spoon was for! I had forgotten all about that," Eleanor said as she took the can. "I like having it just in case of an emergency. A can of Beanie Weenies are the perfect comfort food during an emergency."

"Here they are," Vegas said triumphantly, holding up the keys.

"I knew they were in there," Eleanor said and unlocked her door. "It's nice to open a door that you don't have to ram your shoulder into."

"I'll get your luggage."

"I can do that," Eleanor said. She sat down on the chair in the living room with Pepsi in her lap and quickly fell asleep.

"Sleep it off, tigers," Vegas said with a smile.

Vegas went back to the Volkswagen and got her mother's suitcase out of the trunk. She was grabbing the tools when she saw her mother's phone lying on the passenger side floorboard. She grabbed it and punched in Pepper's number.

"Hello?"

"Pepper, this is Vegas."

"What's wrong?"

"Nothing's wrong. I just got back from Flat Bottom, Georgia."

There was a short pause as if Pepper was trying to figure something out. "Why would anybody go to Flat Bottom, Georgia?"

"It was for my case. The *Riddles and Riches* one. How long have you been home?"

"Big Shelly dropped me off a few hours ago."

"Sorry I woke you. Did you see a Wood Booger?"

"Nah, but we did see a raccoon with a bucket on its head. I went to try and get it off, but it took off running and the bucket came off and he fell into it. Nature can be really odd sometimes. Odd and entertaining."

"Yeah, I always enjoyed watching the raccoon bucket races. Listen, I have the final clue for my case, the one that leads to the treasure. I wanted to see if you know what it means."

"I will do my best."

Vegas fumbled in her pockets until she found her notebook. She opened it up and began reading the final clue. "It says, *Go to the place where the Wood Booger does roam. The swamp is sloppy and through it you must comb.*"

"Well, that's obviously Sloppy Swamp. Parts of it are very sloppy. You should see my pants. I can still smell them and they're outside in a tree."

"Why are they in a tree?"

"It was dark when I got home last night. But Sloppy Swamp is several thousand acres. You'll never be able to find anything without more of a clue than that."

"There is more. *Go to the Morris Tree above the moors. Then the treasure you seek will be yours.*"

"The Morris Tree, I know where that is."

"That's great! But what's a Morris Tree?"

"It's where Butane Morris saw the Wood Booger and filmed it."

"His name was Butane?"

"I guess his parents were fans of fire or something. It's the best footage of a Wood Booger ever filmed. It's even better than the Patterson Film. It's on YouTube if you want to check it out."

"I guess I will. I was talking with a woman about Walter Peabody, she knew him. She said he went off to live in the woods to get away from everybody and she hasn't seen him since. Maybe he went to Sloppy Swamp."

"I don't know if anybody could live there."

"You just spent a couple nights there, didn't you?"

There was a pause on the other end of the line before Pepper said, "There's that."

"I'm at my mother's house right now. I'm going to go home and take a nap. Do you think you could come by my house around noon and take me out to the Morris Tree to have a look around?"

"Sure, Vegas. I'll take you wherever you want to go."

"Great. I'll see you then."

"It's a date."

"No. You're helping me with my case. At best, it's an outing."

"An outing is a date."

"No."

"Okay, it's a shadow date."

"I don't even know what that is."

But before she could get an explanation Pepper had already hung up the phone.

CHAPTER 28

THE SUN SHINING through the small window of Vegas' airstream camper streaked her face like war paint. She came awake slowly as the sound of faint talking entered her ears. She reached instinctively for the alarm radio believing it was on. She sat up when she realized it wasn't. She rubbed her eyes and listened as she stared down at her Scooby Doo sheets.

She couldn't make out what the voices were saying. She pulled the covers down and got up. She was wearing a pair of gray cut-off jogging pants and a shirt that read, "Don't turn around, you're not going that way."

Vegas walked to the door and looked out the small window and saw Pepper and her mother working on the opened passenger side door of the Volkswagen. She stepped outside.

"What are you all doing?" Vegas asked through a large yawn as she shielded the sun from her eyes.

"I'm working on your door," Pepper said as he was doing something with the door lock.

"He's doing a great job, too," Eleanor said. "He got it opened. Here's the handle."

Vegas stared at the proffered item. "You broke my door?"

Pepper replied, "Technically, it was already broken,

because it wouldn't open. So, no, I didn't break your door. I broke the handle."

"He had another handle," said Eleanor. "He's very handy to have around."

Vegas watched Pepper open and close the door several times.

"Why are you opening and closing it now?" asked Vegas.

"I can't get it to shut properly," Pepper informed her.

"Oh, great," Vegas said and threw her hands in the air in despair. "First it wouldn't open, now it won't close. You sold me a piece of junk."

"When you bought the Volkswagen from me, the doors worked fine," Pepper said. "The heater was the only thing messed up."

"I didn't know anything was wrong with the heater."

Pepper was quiet for a second. "Then ignore what I just said."

"Maybe the door is messed up because of a manufacturing flaw of some sort," suggested Eleanor.

"It's messed up because you tried to break into it," Vegas reminded her.

"Why did you try to break into it, Eleanor?" asked Pepper.

"I didn't want her to leave me."

"Why did you want to leave her, Vegas?"

Vegas was annoyed with both of them and decided to ignore the question. "Pepper, can I ask you something?"

"I guess, as long as you're not going to answer my question."

"I asked you to meet me here at around noon, right?"

"Yes. And I am here at noon fixing your door with abandon. I also brought you a present." Pepper went to his truck and got some flowers and handed them to her. "I thought I should bring you something for our shadow date."

"It's not a date," Vegas said and reluctantly took the flowers.

"See, that's what's so great about a shadow date," said Pepper. "You date someone without them knowing it. That way there's no fear of rejection."

"That is brilliant," said Eleanor.

"No, that is odd," Vegas said. "But back to my original point here. I told you to meet me here around noon, but I didn't tell you to bring my mother."

Pepper humped his huge shoulders. "Well, it was on the way here, so I thought I'd stop and ask your mother if she wanted to come."

"I did," Eleanor said with a big smile. She hugged her daughter hard for a few seconds before letting her go. "It's almost like Pepper and me are shadow dating now."

Pepper laughed.

"Mom, don't put that in my head. You should be at home resting," Vegas said. "Aren't you tired?" She set the flowers and door handle on a cinderblock by the Volkswagen.

"Not since I've been doing at-home square dance classes. It's given me some renewed vigor. It comes with a DVD. I bought a dress for it. You should see me in it. I feel forty-five again."

Vegas rolled her eyes before asking, "Where's Pepsi? Did you give him to Pepper?"

"I'm trying to cut down on pop," Pepper said, "but I would take a drink."

"What do you want?" asked Vegas.

"Pop is fine."

"I thought you were cutting back," she said.

"I think we both know that's not happening."

Eleanor chimed in. "Pepsi wasn't a pop. Well, I mean it's a

pop, but this Pepsi was a cat. We found him trapped inside a Pepsi machine in front of a motel, hence his name."

"Interesting," Pepper said.

"Where's he at now?" asked Vegas.

"Who?"

"Pepsi," Vegas groaned. She thought she was going to lose her mind if she had to talk to these two much longer.

"I'm still thirsty, by the way," added Pepper.

"I gave him to the neighbor," Eleanor said. "She has a daughter. I think her name is Marcie. Or was it Thornton? No, Thornton is the other neighbor's son. I didn't know you were coming by, Pepper or I would have offered him to you."

"I don't need any more animals. I had two black labs named Bert and Ernie I had to get rid of because they kept breaking into my refrigerator and making a mess. I had to throw away my good cheese."

"I'll go get you something to drink," Eleanor said.

"Thanks."

"How did your dogs break into your fridge anyway?" asked Vegas.

"They probably called somebody to come and open it for them. They were very persuasive."

Vegas walked to the passenger door and tried to close it, but it wouldn't latch. "How am I going to keep this closed?"

"I'll figure it out," Pepper said.

"I don't have time to do that right now. I want to get to Sloppy Swamp and find the treasure."

"No problem there. I know where the Morris Tree is, so I can take you right to it. I'll take my truck and you can follow me in the Volkswagen. I have a bunch of car parts in the front and back here, so I don't have any room in there or you could ride with me. Although if your mother's coming, it would be a tight squeeze anyway, and I don't know how you feel about that. Do you have anything to dig with?"

"I've got a shovel and a pick ax."

Vegas tried several more times to close the door, but it simply wouldn't latch. "How am I going to get the door to stay closed?"

"Don't worry, I've got some old clothesline in my truck that I used for a dance class."

"What kind of dance uses clothesline?"

"None, apparently. Turns out I read the flier wrong."

The two of them walked to the truck to get the clothesline when Eleanor came out of the Airstream holding a plastic cup filled with water. "Are we going in Pepper's truck?" she shouted.

"No, Mom!" Vegas shouted back. "We aren't going. You're going to stay here and get some rest."

"This girl doesn't miss a chance at adventure."

"Oh, let her come, Vegas," said Pepper.

"Whatever. We'll follow him in the Volkswagen. We're getting his dancing rope to secure the Volkswagen door. You can go on and get in."

"Let me give him his water first," Eleanor said as she walked to Pepper and handed him a blue plastic cup. "Vegas didn't have any pop. How come you didn't have any pop?"

"I don't want any."

"Water is fine," said Pepper.

Pepper drank the water straight down. Eleanor seemed impressed.

"You sure were thirsty. All right, I'll go wait in the vehicle," she said.

Pepper told Vegas, "What should I do with the cup?"

"You can keep it as a memory for this day."

"Thank you," said Pepper, and he threw it in the back of the truck. He found the clothesline rolled up neatly and grabbed it.

As they turned, they saw Eleanor crawling into the driver's side of the Volkswagen.

Pepper asked, "Why is your mother trying to get into the passenger seat by crawling through the driver's side instead of going through the passenger side door that doesn't close?"

Vegas glanced at Pepper, then back at the Volkswagen. "Hey, you brought her."

CHAPTER 29

VEGAS AND ELEANOR followed Pepper as he turned off the highway onto a gravel road. They bumped along for what seemed like an eternity.

"Where is he taking us?" Eleanor asked.

"To Sloppy Swamp."

"I didn't know it was this far."

"Well, Wood Boogers like to be out by themselves, I reckon," mused Vegas.

"Do you believe in Wood Boogers?"

"No. Do you?"

"Apparently so, because I'm out here looking for them."

Vegas shook her head in wonder. "No, Mom, we're not looking for Wood Boogers. We're looking for the Morris Tree to find the treasure."

"Oh, yeah, Mommy remembers now."

Pepper pulled off to the side near a crop of trees at the mouth of a trail. Vegas parked the Volkswagen behind his truck.

"Stay there and I'll untie your door," Vegas said.

"Okay. I feel big time now that my door works!"

"If you call untying it working," Vegas mumbled as she

walked around to the passenger side door. Pepper helped her try to get the knots loose.

"How many knots did you put in this thing?" asked Vegas.

"I didn't want your mother to roll out," Pepper said. They finally got the knots loose and opened the door for Eleanor.

"Watching you all untie me like that made me feel like I was being unwrapped like a big Christmas present," Eleanor said with a hearty laugh.

Vegas said, "Well, you're not what I asked Santa for, but I guess I'll keep you." She addressed Pepper. "Where do we go now?"

"We have to walk about a mile straight up that mountain, and then you hit the swamp," Pepper said as he pointed to the mountain. "The Morris Tree is just a few hundred yards from there, but it's kind of thick to get up there."

"How thick?" asked a concerned Vegas.

"Thick thick is the only way I know how to describe it. But the Morris Tree is in a clearing. The woods open up into this large circular area, and that's where the footage of the Wood Booger was taken. It's almost like holy ground to the Wood Booger community."

Vegas thought about his description. "Why is there a large circular area with a lone tree in it anyway?"

Pepper told her, "Nobody knows for sure, but most of the Wood Booger community believes it's where the aliens landed."

"Aliens?" Vegas and Eleanor said in unison.

Eleanor then rubbed her hands together and smiled. "This is the best vacation ever."

"Mom, this isn't a vacation. Why can't I get that through your head?"

"They have a campsite down the road here, if you all want to spend your vacation here," Pepper said.

"Let's do it!" shouted an enthusiastic Eleanor.

"I have a tent I can let you all use, just make sure the hole is on the bottom," said Pepper.

Vegas shouted, "The case, people! We're here on my case, not to set up vacation plans!"

Pepper said softly, "Sorry. I was just trying to help."

Vegas turned to her mother and told her, "Maybe you should stay here. It sounds like it might be a rough walk."

"But I want to see the aliens," she said with a pout.

Vegas closed her eyes and bowed her head as if she was trying to keep from screaming. She looked back at her mother. "There are no aliens here, Mom. Only crazy people live on this planet."

"I disagree," Pepper said. "We think they come here and talk with the Wood Boogers."

"Aliens talk to the Wood Boogers?" Vegas asked. "I didn't know that Wood Boogers could talk."

"Wood Boogers don't talk to people," said Pepper. "They only talk to the aliens."

Eleanor said, "Well, I've got to see this."

"Do you have your phone with you, Eleanor?" asked Pepper.

"Yes. Are you going to call the aliens?" she asked as she dug through her purse for her phone. "I have some Beanie Weenies I can offer them as a peace offering. Providing, of course, I can find my spoon again."

Pepper told her, "No. I just want to show Miss Doubting Thomas over here the footage of the Wood Booger."

Vegas watched her mother rummaging through her purse. She turned to Pepper and said, "We're going to be here a while."

Eleanor finally located her phone and showed it off like a

prized pig at the county fair. "I found it! I knew it was in there. Mommy knows what she's doing sometimes."

Pepper took the phone and began looking for the Wood Booger footage as Eleanor and Vegas gathered around the small screen. "Here it is," Pepper said. "The reception isn't the best here, but it's loading. Here we go. Now look at this footage, and tell me there's no such thing as a Wood Booger."

Vegas rolled her eyes, while Eleanor clapped excitedly.

"That's a genuine Wood Booger filmed right on top of this mountain at the Morris Tree," Pepper said proudly.

"That is the most fascinating thing I've ever seen in my life," said Eleanor. "And I've seen a lot of fascinating things."

Vegas observed, "It looks like a guy in a gorilla suit."

Pepper shook his head. "That's what a Wood Booger looks like, Vegas. You have to open the science side of your mind every now and then."

"The science side of my mind says that's a guy in a gorilla suit. I am a woman of true science. Now take me to where the aliens landed."

"Let's grab the tools and head up," Pepper said. They got the shovel and pick ax, then walked through laurel patches, over boulders, across mountain streams, and finally up a steep embankment until they got to the clearing.

To the right was a smelly, thick swamp encircled with trees. Bugs flew all about. To the left, in the center of the clearing, was a lone tree.

"That's the famous Morris Tree," Pepper said.

"It definitely looks the way you described it," said Vegas.

The three of them made their way to the tree and stopped. Vegas began looking around for any evidence of the treasure. Eleanor appeared more fascinated with the circle.

"So this is where the aliens landed?" she asked.

"This is the place. They say if you relax that you can hear the aliens talking to you in your mind. You should try that."

"Oh, I'll get to use my new skills as a clairvoyant," Eleanor said. She excitedly rubbed her hands together in anticipation of a possible life-altering event. She then placed her index fingers on the sides of her temples and closed her eyes and attempted to talk with the aliens. "Aliens from afar, can you put a thought into my head?"

"A book can't even do that," Vegas chimed in.

Eleanor opened her eyes and watched her daughter shovel into a patch of ground. "You disrupted my thought process, Vegas."

"Now you know how I feel," Vegas said as she tossed aside a shovelful of dirt.

Vegas raised the shovel high and plunged it into the ground. All three of them heard a clunk, and all three of them smiled in anticipation of what they might have just found.

"Is that the treasure?" Eleanor squealed.

"I'm not sure," Vegas said. "I didn't think I would hit it so soon."

"It has to be," said Pepper. "There's no other thing I could think of that might be buried up here."

Vegas dug frantically until she tired herself out, at which point Pepper used the pick ax. After a half-hour of digging, they uncovered a box about six feet long and four feet wide.

"This has to be it," said Vegas. "I wonder why it's so big."

"There's a lot of treasure in it," Eleanor said.

"Take some pictures, Mom."

"I'm on it," Eleanor said as she searched inside her purse for her phone.

"Did you lose the phone already?" Vegas asked in a frustrated voice.

"It's not considered lost until you scream," Eleanor said. "Aha!"

"Sounds like you screamed anyway," said Vegas.

"I was excited."

Eleanor started to take pictures, but Pepper stopped her. "Let me try and clean up a little

before you take my picture."

"I don't believe you're supposed to be in the pictures, Pepper," said Vegas.

"Let him be in the pictures, Vegas," Eleanor said. "I mean, he showed us where the treasure was to start with."

"I solved the clues," said Vegas.

"But you didn't know what a Morris Tree was," said Pepper.

"I would have figured it out eventually," Vegas said.

"I don't think you would have. Maybe Eleanor and I should start our own detective club."

"That would be so much fun," Eleanor said excitedly. "We could call it Sherlock's Warriors."

"I love that name," Pepper said.

"It's not a detective club," Vegas said. "Oh, never mind. We'll argue the merits of your enterprise later. Right now let's just get the lid opened."

Vegas placed the tip of the shovel under the lip of the lid and lifted up. When that didn't do it, Pepper took the pick ax and helped her. "Go team, go team, go team," Eleanor chanted.

Vegas stopped prying and looked at her mother. "What are you doing?"

"I'm encouraging you. I'm a detective cheerleader."

"Go team, go team, go team," Pepper echoed.

"Would you two stop cheering?" shouted Vegas. "We need to focus on getting this lid off."

"You're right, Vegas," said a contrite Eleanor. "My mind,

body, and soul are focused on getting this lid off. Pepper, you've got a hole in your pants. I've got a sewing kit in my purse here. Vegas, come up here and help Mommy find it."

"That's not being focused, Mom."

"She is right though," Pepper said as he examined the hole in his pants. "I think I got it caught on a nail when I was trying to get my foot out of the commode."

Vegas stared at him silently for a moment, wondering if she should ask the question she didn't know if she wanted the answer to. "Why was your foot in the commode?"

"Who's unfocused now?" asked Eleanor.

"Not now, cheerleader captain," Vegas said. "Pepper, how did you get your foot into the commode?"

"I was cleaning and I was going to step on the commode to knock down some spiderwebs, but the lid was up when I thought it was down, and I stepped right in it. It scared me to death. I thought I was falling through the floor."

"Why would you need to stand on a commode? You're ten feet tall."

"I have a high ceiling in the bathroom. But I'll definitely put the lid down from now on."

Vegas shook her head and turned her attention back to the treasure box lid. After a few more minutes of struggle, they finally got enough of the lid loose. They grinned at each other.

"We're just inches from seeing the treasure," said a giddy Eleanor. "I haven't been this excited since I won that squash at Food City."

"I once won a belt at the county fair," Pepper said. "It didn't fit though."

Vegas looked at Pepper and her mother. "I really wish I had a team that would stay focused."

"It's not always about you, Vegas," Eleanor replied.

Vegas shook her head and put her hands on the lid. "Here goes." She lifted the lid and pushed it to the side.

The three of them looked into the box with confused horror. Inside wasn't treasure but the skeletal remains of a human body.

"That's the stupidest treasure ever," Eleanor said.

"Someone's been murdered," Vegas said.

Then a voice called out, "And somebody is about to be murdered again."

Vegas, Eleanor, and Pepper looked to their right and saw Davis Harper standing with his arms crossed and a wicked grin on his face. He was flanked on each side by Squirrel and Skunk Snodgrass, who were holding shotguns.

Eleanor whispered, "I should have stayed at the vehicle. I also wish I got that table at Walmart."

CHAPTER 30

VEGAS, Eleanor and Pepper were tied to separate trees on the outside edge of the circle of where the Morris Tree stood. Davis Harper was on his cellphone some distance away from them. Skunk and Squirrel were trying to feed them Moon Pies.

"We were wondering if you all might be hungry," Squirrel said.

Vegas replied angrily, "Hungry? I don't think hunger is at the top of my list right now."

"I'm kind of hungry," said Eleanor.

"Me too," said Pepper.

Squirrel took out a Moon Pie, pulled open the plastic, and fed Eleanor while Skunk did the same with Pepper.

"I can't believe you two are eating at a time like this," fumed Vegas. "They've got us tied to trees, for crying out loud. We shouldn't trust them."

After Eleanor was fed, Squirrel took out another Moon Pie and offered it to Vegas. "Are you sure you don't want one?" he asked.

"No, I don't want one. You all are going to kill us, aren't you? Because I figured out your plan. Mr. Harper robbed the treasure long ago and sold it to help pay off all of his gambling debts, but there was money left over and he gambled it all away, too. So he had to sell off his publishing company, but the company that was going to buy him out wanted to see the treasure because of the rumors that it wasn't real. He hired me thinking I'd never find it. But I did."

Eleanor then said, "Can I have her Moon Pie?"

"Mom!" Vegas yelled in frustration.

"I can't help it," Eleanor said. "I'm still hungry."

Vegas addressed Squirrel as Skunk fed Eleanor another snack. "You're going to kill us like you did Peabody."

"Is that who is in that box?" Eleanor asked through a mouth full of Moon Pie.

Vegas stared at her mother in disbelief. "Who did you think it was?"

"I didn't know."

Pepper interrupted. "I can't hear what Eleanor is saying. Can you tell me?"

"It's kind of hard to tell what she's saying with her mouth full," Vegas said.

"Can I get another Moon Pie?" asked Pepper.

"You two get over here!" shouted Mr. Harper. Squirrel and Skunk hurried to him.

Eleanor looked at her purse in puzzlement, then whispered, "Oh, my phone is vibrating. For a moment, I thought Pepsi was in there."

"Can you reach the phone?" Vegas asked.

"I'll try."

"What did Eleanor say?" asked Pepper.

"She's vibrating."

Pepper was quiet for a moment, then said, "I don't even know how to respond to that."

Eleanor managed to get one arm free from the ropes. She

reached out and got her purse, then began searching for her phone.

"I know it's in here," she whispered.

"Would you hurry and find it," Vegas urged.

"Here it is," said Eleanor. She answered the phone and whispered, "Hello? Oh, hi, Martha." She looked at Vegas. "It's Martha."

"Tell her to call the police," Vegas pleaded through gritted teeth.

"What have you been doing, Martha? Oh, I hate to hear that. I read on the internet if you soak it in pudding, the swelling will go down."

"Mother," Vegas whispered angrily.

"Oh, I'm sorry. You better go tend to them beans then. Bye."

Vegas stared at her mother, utterly perplexed. Eleanor looked at her daughter and realized her mistake. "I should have told her we were tied up, shouldn't I?"

"Yes, you should have."

"She was cooking a kettle of green beans and the water started boiling over, so she had to go. I guess I should have started with the tied up thing first. I hope her swelling goes down. I wonder if I told her about soaking it in pudding."

"You told her that," Vegas whispered.

Eleanor smiled. "I feel better now."

Vegas shook her head in frustration. "Great. Can you call 911?"

"Sure. Uh, do you have to dial the area code first when you call 911?"

"No."

"What did Eleanor say?" asked Pepper.

"She wanted to know if you have to dial the area code."

"That's a strange thing to ask when you're tied up," he said.

"I'm not getting a signal now," Eleanor said as she fiddled with the phone. "Hold on. ... Excuse me!" she yelled to Mr. Harper, Squirrel, and Skunk.

"What are you doing?" Vegas whispered in a panic.

"I'm going to ask them if they'll tie us up on the other side of the alien landing zone so I can get a signal."

Davis Harper stared hard at his three captives and walked over to Eleanor angrily. He ripped the phone from her hand and threw it to the side. "You're not calling anybody!"

Squirrel took out his box of treats and asked, "Do you all want another Moon Pie?"

"I do." said Eleanor.

"You've already had two," said Vegas.

"I'm still hungry," said Eleanor.

Squirrel tore open a Moon Pie and was about to give it to Eleanor when Mr. Harper stopped him. "Why are you feeding her my Moon Pies?"

"She seems to like 'em," Squirrel said.

"I don't want you feeding them," Mr. Harper said angrily and yanked the box out of Squirrel's hands and threw them as far as he could.

"I don't understand," Skunk said.

Vegas saw her opening to divide the trio. "He's going to kill us like he did Peabody," she said.

Squirrel and Skunk looked stunned.

"We don't want to kill anybody," Squirrel said. "You said they were stealing from you and you wanted to teach them a lesson. You didn't say anything about killing them."

"What did we steal?" asked Eleanor.

"We didn't steal anything," said Vegas.

"What did Eleanor say?" asked Pepper.

"She wanted to know what we stole, but we didn't steal anything."

"I'm relieved," said Pepper.

Mr. Harper looked at Vegas. "I have to admit you're smarter than I thought you were. The only reason I hired you for this job is because I was convinced you wouldn't figure out the clues. In fact, I didn't think anybody would ever figure it out."

"Never underestimate a mother and daughter team," Eleanor said proudly.

Mr. Harper looked at Eleanor and Pepper and told Vegas, "I think your team is as stupid as mine."

"I don't disagree with you there," she said.

"Well, I guess you already know how this ends," Mr. Harper said with an evil grin on his face.

"You can't kill us," said Vegas. "What will you tell the publishing company that wants to buy you out?"

"I'll just give them the clues you found to prove they're real, then tell them I confirmed the treasure. That should placate them enough to go through with the deal."

"You don't even know what the clues are," said Vegas.

"They're on my phone," said Eleanor.

"Mom, you're not helping."

Mr. Harper laughed. "Why did you think I wanted you to record the coordinates? Now, I believe we need to bring this conversation to an end."

He pulled out a revolver from a shoulder holster beneath his suit jacket. As he did, a voice shouted, "Hold it right there!"

Vegas turned and saw Sergeant Miller standing with his gun drawn and a team of police officers behind him. Mr. Harper, Skunk, and Squirrel all lifted their hands in surrender. Mr. Harper was disarmed, and Sergeant Miller untied Vegas, Eleanor, and Pepper.

"How did you find us?" Vegas asked as she rubbed her hands and wrists to try and get the blood flowing again.

"I put a trace on your cellphone when you told me the guy

driving the truck following you was different from the one it was registered to. I did some detective work of my own and found out that Mr. Harper was deep in debt and needing funds, so I thought you might be in trouble and in need of some help. I think that a lot, by the way."

Vegas smiled. "You worried about me. I'm touched." She then noticed her mother was eating another Moon Pie. "How many of those things are you going to eat?"

"Until the box is empty, I'm guessing," Eleanor said after she swallowed another mouthful.

Vegas turned back to Sergeant Miller. "I need to take all the information I gathered for the *Riddles and Riches* puzzle and give it to the publisher that was going to purchase his company."

"I already called the publisher of the company," said Sergeant Miller.

"How did you know who to call?"

"I'm a detective," Sergeant Miller said matter-of-factly. "His name is Dalton Summers. He's on his way now to headquarters so we can talk. I told him about my suspicions and about your investigation, and he told me that he would make sure you got paid."

"That's good to know. There's a body over there in that box. I'm guessing it's Walter Peabody."

"I'll get a coroner up here to get the body. Do you know the next of kin?"

"I don't believe there is a next of kin. He just wanted to be by himself."

"I'm glad you're safe, Miss Chantly," Sergeant Miller said as he pulled out his cellphone to report back to headquarters.

Vegas turned to Pepper. "Thanks for your help."

"Any time, Vegas."

"Are you ready to go, Mom?"

"Just give me a few seconds. I'm too full to move right now."

"Mom, I love you. I really do. But you're the strangest person I know."

"You helped make me this way," Eleanor said as she retrieved her phone.

As they began the hike back to their yellow Volkswagen, Vegas took her mother's hand. "You know, this was a pretty good vacation after all."

ABOUT THE AUTHOR

Kyle Owens lives in the Appalachian Mountains. His stories have appeared in Ahoy Comics, Eastern Iowa Review, 2228, among others and several anthologies. His comic strip, "Pop and Fries the Awesome Guys!" appears in the quarterly magazine "Adventures" out of Ohio. His husband-and-wife Christmas romantic comedy "A Mountain Christmas Wedding" was published by Books to Go Now. His cartoon collection. "The New Yorker Hates My Cartoons" was published by Clash Books.

To learn more about Kyle Owens and discover more Next Chapter authors, visit our website at www.nextchapter.pub.

Riddles & Riches
ISBN: 978-4-82419-721-4

Published by
Next Chapter
2-5-6 SANNO
SANNO BRIDGE
143-0023 Ota-Ku, Tokyo
+818035793528

30th August 2024

Milton Keynes UK
Ingram Content Group UK Ltd.
UKHW030750221024
449869UK00004B/229

9 784824 197214